THREE LIONS ROAR

THREE LIONS ROAR

A Novel Of World Cup 2006

Umut Ozturk

iUniverse, Inc.
New York Lincoln Shanghai

Three Lions Roar
A Novel Of World Cup 2006

iUniverse books may be ordered through booksellers or by contacting:

iUniverse
2021 Pine Lake Road, Suite 100
Lincoln, NE 68512
www.iuniverse.com
1-800-Authors (1-800-288-4677)

ISBN-13: 978-0-595-36112-0 (pbk)
ISBN-13: 978-0-595-82356-7 (cloth)
ISBN-13: 978-0-595-80555-6 (ebk)
ISBN-10: 0-595-36112-9 (pbk)
ISBN-10: 0-595-82356-4 (cloth)
ISBN-10: 0-595-80555-8 (ebk)

Printed in the United States of America

For the true inspirations of my life:

My mother and father

Acknowledgments

❀

This book is dedicated to all those great players that I have ever had the honor to coach at the Biloxi Soccer Organization. This includes all of the wonderful kids that I coached starting from 1995 and all the way until 2002. Thank you for all the great memories. I would like to thank USSF "C" Licenced coaches Kanat and Bulut Ozturk for making this book a reality. Rain, I love you.

I would also like to take a moment and thank some extraordinary people that have made my writing possible in this great country of ours. If you know me at all I must admit I don't have many friends. I could count my best friends on one hand. First and foremost my mentor Steve Colbet, thank you for all of your guidance. Second, my friend Casey Taylor, thank you for making this book possible. I don't have to say anything else to you, Casey, you should know what I mean. Third, Brian Brazil, thank you for listening to me whine when things don't go right. You are a true pal.

Last but not least, I would like to thank all of my high school teachers from Biloxi High School. They knew me when I couldn't put a coherent sentence together in English. Thank you for being patient with my quest to learn the English language. I must tell the whole world if you want your child to be educated by the most outstanding teachers in America, then you definitely have to send your child to Biloxi High School.

Foreword

❦

I walked into an indoor soccer arena somewhere in the suburbs of north St. Paul to play soccer with Umut, his brother, Bulut, and a gang of their uncles and cousins. I've never been much of a soccer player, basketball's my sport, but I agreed to give this a shot. I wasn't as scared as I was nervous. I knew Umut and Bulut were both trying out for the Minnesota Thunder, our professional soccer team here in Minnesota, in about a month. Needless to say, I was quite intimidated. Before we left Umut's house, I asked him if he had any extra shin guards for me. "No, you don't need them." I believed him. I'm such a sucker. We rode from Umut's and Bulut's house with one of their cousins. It was late, after midnight. We were the first to arrive and headed to the locker room. As I'm putting on my basketball shorts—I didn't have any soccer shorts because I don't play soccer—I look over and see all three of them strapping on their shin guards! "What the hell!? I thought you didn't need shin guards!?"

Their dirty smiles told me I did. "Umut! What the hell!? Do you have any extra ones for me?" "No," he said with his stupid accent. "Look in the lockers, sometimes people leave stuff behind by accident." Now I was scared. I was about to go play soccer with a couple of wannabe pros and I don't have any damn shin guards! I knew good and well that there were no shin guards that would magically pop out of a locker, but I looked anyway. Annoyed and scared for the safety of my shins, I did the next best thing I could think of. I started stuffing socks into the knee high soccer socks that Bulut had lent me. "What the hell are you doing?" Umut asked. Some people say there are no stupid questions but I disagree. That was a stupid question.

"What do you think I'm doing? I'm not about to go out there and let my shins get pounded. I need some protection." They were all laughing by now. I have to admit, by the time I was done stuffing my socks, like a twelve year old girl stuffs her bra, it looked pretty funny. I wasn't about to take them out though, no way. We walked out onto the field. It was big, and I knew I wasn't in any kind of shape to be running up and down it all night, or should I say, morning. I found my calling, goaltender! Very little running but it held it's own frightening setbacks, namely soccer balls kicked hard, directly at me and my fragile face, and more importantly, genitalia. I weighed my options and decided my reflexes should be good enough to avoid a total disaster so I decided to give goal keeping my best shot. After fielding a few practice shots from these former high school soccer stars I got a little more comfortable. That's when the trash talking started. "I thought you played soccer, Umut? I'm pretty sure you haven't gotten one past me yet, you girl." With a smile and a laugh he responded, "It's because we're shooting from a quarter field away, you fruitcake." "No, it's because you have a weak leg, and I'm to quick for you," I taunted. Just then, Bulut railed one into the upper corner of the net. I yelled, "that one doesn't count, I wasn't watching. Who shoots at someone who isn't looking anyway? Cut your hair, Bulut, you look like a girl, and Umut plays like a girl. I guess that's why you're brothers, huh." I always find it best to trash talk when you're really not good at something, if anything, it's a weak attempt at intimidation. It usually doesn't work but it keeps things friendly in my mind, otherwise I can get a little to competitive sometimes. They continued shooting from a safe distance, and I continued running my mouth. They were nice enough to loan me some goalkeeper gloves, which helped immensely.

After a little while, four or five of their uncles showed up. I guess not everyone came that was supposed to, so we decided to move to one of the smaller fields. I liked this idea at first before realizing that closer quarters meant closer shots. The game started with about four people on each side. I stuck out like a soar thumb. A tall gangly white guy in a group of all Turkish people. A few of them hardly spoke any English but I didn't need to understand them to know when they were making fun of the boobs I had implanted in my socks, which were all bunched up by now and looking even funnier than before. I was nervous again as the game began and was completely busted when the first shot came from midfield. I bent down to field it only to have it slip right through my legs and into the goal. Haha, serves me right for all that trash talking I was doing earlier. It was quite funny, it was the easiest shot I would face all night, and I let it roll right through my legs. First shot jitters, I guess. After that I settled down. I was impressed with myself and how well I did. At one point, Umut and another member of his team broke away and were heading right for me, Umut handling the ball. Oh shit, I thought to myself. At this point that was really the thing that scared me the most, break away's. As they approached I tried to cut off Umut's angle and prepare for the pass I was expecting. They got closer, and Umut maintained control. I moved up to meet him. Right at the top of the crease I slid my legs into his passing lane and put my body in front of the open net. He shot, directly into my stomach. I grabbed it and popped up, looking for an open man to pass to. "Fuck!" Umut yelled. It felt great. I waited until the game was over to let him know just how gifted I am physically and how superior I am to him. At least that's what I said, but it doesn't make it true. After about two hours we called it quits. I was beat and longing for my bed. There was no question in my mind I would be hurting the next day. Everyone thanked me for coming and congratulated me for my efforts. I was pleased with my performance overall and was glad that I came, no shin guards and all.

Casey Taylor

CHAPTER 1

❀

Introduction

Gone were the glory days of Charlton, Moore and Banks. A new breed of footballers had replaced the good old days of English football. Now England had flamboyance and panache. It had been forty years since England had won the cup. Was 2006 World Cup in Germany England's year? Before the World Cup Germany had started, according to many football pundits, England did not have a chance. Football experts thought England would choke like at all the previous World Cups. On this July night before England's first World Cup finals appearance in forty years, those non-believers had become believers. World Cup Germany had created a new English phenomenon. His name is Josh Roark.

CHAPTER 2

❀

Suicide

Josh Roark was born on October 11, 1980, into a poor family in the Northumberland village of Ashington. Josh was the only child of John and Katie Roark. John and Katie were not your typical young parents. John Roark was thirty-five years old and Katie ten years his junior. They had been married four years earlier and had been trying for a child every since. The first four years of their marriage were very tough. They both wanted kids and not being able to procreate caused John to go mad in more than several occasions over the years. John would go to a bar on many nights with friends and get drunk. He would come home and beat on his young bride for not being able to give him a son. Katie would not fight back. She knew it was her fault. Six years earlier, at age nineteen, she had an abortion. In Katie's mind not being able to get pregnant was God's way of punishing her. With the years passing by, John's alcohol abuse started to get more intolerable. He would drink more every night and then come home to use Katie's face as a punching bag.

The third year of their marriage, things got worse around the Roark household. John had been a bartender for the last ten years. Katie had met him at his bar. During that first meeting she had fallen for him. John was an expert on his liquor and especially his whiskey. He had a certain confidence and charm about himself that the opposite sex found attractive. He had been known around Ashington for his two loves: one was his love for football and two, his love for the alcohol bottle. For a drunk, being a bartender was a paradox. After many different fights and many different hangovers, John had promised Katie he would quit drinking if she ever gave him a son.

In the past, Katie had insisted to John on going to a local doctor to find out what was wrong with them. Why couldn't they have kids? Was it her fault? Was it because of the abortion she had years earlier? Was she too old? Surely not! She wanted to find out the source of the problem. Katie would cry herself to sleep many lonely nights when her husband was at his bar getting plastered. Everyday was the same with John. He would drink and then come home to throw a couple of left hooks to his wife's face. Katie wanted an end to her meaningless life. She hated her husband and she hated herself for not being able to bring a life into this world.

On November 3, 1979, after the worst beating of her life, Katie picked up her husband's handgun and decided to end her life. Katie put the gun in her mouth. Tears rolled down from her bruised eyes. Her beautiful face now looked like an old leather football. Her husband's gun was in her mouth fully cocked. Katie pulled the trigger. Nothing had happened when the gun snapped. Katie pulled the gun out of her mouth and looked at it with amazement. Why wasn't she dead? Why couldn't she kill herself? Was God playing another nasty joke on her? She inspected the gun and found that the chamber was empty. There were no bullets in it. Katie started laughing hysterically. Her nerves were out of place. While crying, she wondered to herself, did God want me alive? If so! Why? She hated John Roark. She could not live with him anymore. She could not take the beatings. She could not take the mental abuse. She could not take his drunkenness. Katie decided on the day of her failed suicide attempt that she would give him a son but it would not be his. That next day Katie left Ashington to go stay with her mother at Bedlington.

CHAPTER 3

❀

World Cup 2002

Three Lions had been a struggling football nation to its followers for the past forty years. Expectations were very high every year. Every four years fans of England were ready for English domination to return. Fathers and grand fathers wanted the glory days of 1966.

World Cup 2002 in Korea/Japan was another continuing example of England's inability to win the cup. This was one of the better teams England had put together over the years. In 2002, England's flamboyant superstar Beckham was their captain. England was placed at Group D. Group D was given the name of "The Group of Death," that England and Sweden had to go through at the expense of powerful Argentina and very dangerous Nigeria team. The most hotly anticipated match of the entire opening stage was perhaps the Argentina versus England rematch in Sapporo, Japan. The English captain, Beckham, who was sent off in the previous match between the two teams at France '98, was successfully able put his ghosts to rest, as his penalty kick was the only goal in this fascinating confrontation between the two football kingdoms. England was a happy nation for a couple days; however, their joy was a short lived one. Later on in the tournament they would run straight into a roadblock. It was the eventual World Cup champion, Brazil. Ronaldinho was the conquering Brazilian hero on that day. He had joined a distinguished list of South American football icons. He had torched the English defense for two goals, just like another South American enemy, Maradona. Three Lions fans would forever hate these two players until England won another cup.

CHAPTER 4

❁

Long Walks

Katie's aging mother and father were surprised to see their daughter on that winter evening at their doorstep. Her mother and father were not happy with the condition their daughter was in. Both eyes were swollen, and her lip was busted. Katie's father, Henry, seeing his only daughter like this became very angry.

Henry, holding his daughter's hand, "what the hell are you doing to John?"

Katie, in amazement, "what do you mean? I am not doing anything to him."

Henry, holding her hand tighter, "you must be doing something to him. No human being can get this angry for no reason."

Katie was crying now, "he is a fucking drunk father. I have not done anything to him."

Henry pulled his daughter closer and held her as she cried, "do you want me to kill him?"

Katie was laughing and crying at the same time, "no, father! No, it is my fault."

Katie's mother, Mary, intervened to her daughter's final statement, "no, Katie, it is not your fault. He is the one with the problems. He is a drunk. If we believed in divorce then we would tell you to leave him. But you know we don't believe in divorce. He is your husband for richer and for poorer."

Katie, still hugging Henry, looked at her mother, "I know, mother, I know."

That night Katie went to sleep in her childhood room. While she lay in her bed looking at the ceiling, she couldn't remember the last time she was free. She knew she had to leave that drunk. But she did not know how.

She stayed with Henry and Mary for three weeks. She had not heard from John at all during that time. She did not care. John could be dead as far as Katie was concerned. On her second week in Bedlington she befriended a young eighteen-year old Englishman. His name was Robbie Kiel. She had met Robbie during her long walks through Bedlington. During these walks Katie would be gone for hours. These long walks made Katie feel as if she was a free bird.

After she had met Robbie she had invited this young Englishman that same night to a bar. He was still a boy. Robbie was tall, lanky and had an ambition to be the next great English football star. After hanging out with Robbie at the bar, Katie had told Robbie about her daily walks through the Bedlington countryside. She told him the exact times of her walks. She did not know why she had told him this but she did not care. That is how she had met him. Part of her wanted Robbie to come along for those long walks. For some reason, Katie enjoyed his company. He also seemed to enjoy hers. The next two weeks, Katie spent a lot of time with Robbie. She really liked him. Everyday for two weeks Robbie accompanied Katie on her long journeys through Bedlington. They would talk during these expeditions.

Katie, "what do you want out of life, Robbie?

Robbie, "I want to play football for Manchester United and lead England back to a World Cup championship. Do you think I am crazy?"

Katie, "no, not at all. I think you can do whatever you put your mind to, Robbie."

Robbie smiling, "I know."

Katie, "why are you smiling?"

Robbie, "for a second you sounded like my mother."

Katie laughing now, "I am sorry."

Robbie still smiling, "no problem!"

One Friday night returning home from one of her customary walks with Robbie Katie's mother had given her daughter the news, "we have word from your husband, he wants you back home in Ashington tomorrow night."

Katie, "I don't care what he wants. I am never going back to that drunk."

Her father turned to Katie; "he is your husband. You have to go back."

Mary reinforced what her husband said, "you are a grown woman, Katie, and you have to go back. You can't stay here forever. Do you know what people would say if you have a divorce?"

Katie, "I don't care about what people think. I hate him. I don't love him. He will kill me if I go back. I don't know how much more of John I can handle."

Henry grabbed a hold of his crying daughter's hand, "we love you, but you have to go back."

Katie knew she had to go back as well. But before she went to sleep that night she had to find Robbie. She had to tell him she was leaving. She had to say goodbye. That night, around eleven, she went by Robbie's house. The lights were off. Katie knew which one was Robbie's window. From twelve yards out, she threw a small rock at the window. Perfect throw, strike one! Katie hoped no one heard the noise. She thought to herself, while throwing the second rock, it would be embarrassing if someone saw her here. What would people say? What would people think? Katie was scared. Strike two! With the second rock Robbie still had not answered. Katie decided to leave. As she turned around and walked away, she started crying. She knew in her heart that she would never see Robbie Kiel again. She felt as if she were a kid when she spent time around him. He had made her feel like a teenager again. She had not seen this kind of attention from a man in four years, and she knew she would not see it again for a long time.

Katie walked in her tears through the cold night not realizing Robbie was running behind her quietly. Robbie, "Katie, wait."

Katie turned around, "oh my gosh, I am sorry I have woken you up this late."

Robbie, "don't worry about it. Why are you crying?"

Katie acted like she did not here his question; "did I wake your family?"

Robbie, "no! Why are you crying? Are you okay?"

Katie wiped her tears; "I am okay. I have to go back to Ashington."

Robbie, changing the subject, "you know, my hero Bobby Charlton was born in Ashington."

Katie, "I know, you told me millions of times. Bobby Charlton is my husband's hero as well."

Robbie, "one day I will meet Mr. Charlton."

Katie, knowing Robbie's infatuation with Charlton, "I know, Robbie. You will meet him, and you too will be great like Charlton. You are destined for greatness, Robbie. Always remember that. You are destined to achieve all of your dreams. Don't ever let someone stop you from chasing what is yours. Promise me that you will always try to capture your dreams. Promise me you won't ever become miserable like me."

Robbie, "I promise Katie. I will always chase my dreams. I won't stop until I get there. When do you have to leave?"

Katie still crying, "promise me again!"

Robbie, "I promise Katie. When do you leave?"

Katie, "tomorrow morning."

Robbie, "why?"

Katie, "my husband wants me back."

Robbie, with innocence only a child could possess, "I thought you hated your husband."

Katie responded, "I do."

Robbie, again with the same childish innocence, "don't go, stay with me."

Katie smiled at him and said, "you are too cute."

Robbie, "just stay here. We could be together forever."

Katie smiled and said, "if I stay, you won't ever be able to chase your dreams. I will hold you back. I will make you miserable like myself."

Robbie, "I love you, Katie. Please stay!"

Katie was flattered. Her heart started pounding. At that statement Katie pushed Robbie against a tree, leaned forward, and put her beautiful lips on his. Young Robbie responded. They were kissing more passionately each second. Logic and reason had left Katie. She did not care if anyone saw them kissing. She did not care that she was married. It was too dark for anyone to see them anyway. Robbie started kissing Katie's neck and started slowly going down south. Katie pulled Robbie's pants down as fast as she could. Robbie put his cold hands under her dress and started feeling her womanhood while she did the same to his manhood. Her panties were gone now. Robbie was trying to get inside of this gorgeous older woman. But he did not know how. Katie stopped him. Pushed him back a little and then guided him into her slowly. He had officially become a man. When they were done young Robbie was shaking tremendously. It was the most intense five minutes of both of their lives.

CHAPTER 5

Pregnant

Katie had been back in Ashington for a little over month now. Her husband had kept his promise and not laid a hand on her since her return. John was trying to quit drinking, but it was too hard.

One night Katie turned to John, "if you really want to quit drinking, I think you have to quit tending bar."

John responded, "I will quit drinking but I won't quit my job."

Katie thought this was ludicrous, "John as long as you are a bartender, you can't quit drinking."

John knew she was right, "that is crazy, woman. I have self-discipline. I can quit booze when I want."

Katie laughed inside quietly and said what she was thinking out loud, "what a crock of shit!"

John became angry, "don't make me take off my belt, woman."

Katie did not say anything. She knew she had gotten under his skin. During the month of February in 1980, Katie started getting sick. She was having morning sickness and her breasts were constantly sore. She began to wonder, am I pregnant? Can this be true? Why did I blame myself all those years? It was not my fault that I couldn't have a kid. It was my drunken husband's fault. Katie went to the doctor, and she was told the good news.

Doctor Jones, "Mrs. Roark, you are pregnant."

Katie in tears, "are you sure, Doctor?"

Doctor Jones, "as sure as one can be."

Katie had tears of joy coming out of her eyes, "thank you, Doctor."

Doctor Jones, "I will let you talk to my nurse, and I need you to come back in the next several months."

Katie, "thank you, Doctor."

That day Katie went home and decided to make a new room for the baby. All her prayers had been answered. There was nothing wrong with her. Katie wondered to herself, God was not punishing me after all. John came home from work very late that evening. He was being really rowdy and obnoxious outside the house. Katie realized he was drunk again and ran into her room and locked her door.

John came into the house as drunk as a three-dollar bill, "where the hell are you, Katie?"

Katie did not respond.

John, screaming now, "come out, and serve your husband, woman."

Katie responded loudly behind the closed wooden door; "I am not coming out!"

John started beating on her door; "come out now, or I will take my belt out."

Katie screamed back from behind the door, "I am not coming out!"

John went crazy. Punching the door harder and harder, "come out now or else!"

Katie screamed back from behind the door; "or else what, you drunken bastard. I am not going to let you beat on me anymore. If you lay another hand on me ever again I will kill you in your sleep. I am pregnant you bastard. I am carrying your son."

John was too drunk to comprehend what she had said; "what? What did you say?"

Katie screamed back louder; "I am pregnant you asshole! I won't come out until you sober up. I won't let you beat on me and lose my son!"

John was silenced! "I love you, Katie. Open the door."

Katie screamed again, "not until you sober up, you drunk bastard."

John sat by the door smiling and said to the brown wooden door, "I love you, Katie. I knew for all these years that it was not my fault. I knew one day you would give me a son. I will teach him how to play football and make him the next Bobby Charlton. England will be proud of my son, Josh Roark."

Katie quietly said, "good night. I am going to sleep. The baby and I need rest."

John smiling at the door, "I love you, baby. I will be quiet."

With that statement John slipped into a state of unconsciousness. Katie was very happy that John had left her alone that night. She was also shocked to hear him say that he loved her. That was the first time she had heard him say those words in four years.

CHAPTER 6

❀

Football Prodigy

Josh Roark was born on October 11, 1980 in Ashington. John was ecstatic when he found out he had a new baby boy.

John to Katie, "I love you, baby. I knew you were going to give me a boy."

Katie, in tears staring at her son, Josh, and ignoring John, "I love you, little Josh."

John turned to his son; "little Josh, you are going to be the greatest football player to ever come out of Ashington. You know something, my little buddy, you have the same birthday as my hero Bobby Charlton. He will be your hero too."

During Katie's pregnancy John had promised to not drink anymore. But to Katie his promises did not mean anything. He had promised millions of times before and had found a way to waver from his promises. To Katie, John would always be a drunk. She knew a leopard could never change its spots. It had been almost nine months, and John had not touched a liquor bottle. On the day Josh was born, John made a promise to his wife, "I will never drink a drop of liquor, and I will never a lay a hand on you again." Katie just smiled back at him and hoped he would keep his promises. She knew she had warned John during her pregnancy and made her point clear that if he hit her again, she would leave him.

The first toy little Josh ever received was a little football. He was two weeks old. During the next several years, before John would go to work he would take little Josh with him to football stores. There he would buy his little boy all kinds of football items. Josh's room had become a shrine to English football. There were Manchester United flags all over the room. There was a picture of Bobby Charlton hanging right over his crib. John thought if he looked at the greatest soccer player England has ever produced every time he opened and closed his eyes, then he will be like Charlton. There were also other posters in the room. A poster of Gordon Banks hung at little Josh's door, as well as framed Bobby Moore newspaper clippings placed right next to the Charlton posters. These three players had been John's heroes for all of his life. Now they were going to be his son's heroes.

Katie, "John, you are insane. You are buying him too many football items. What if he does not want to play football?"

John apparently never thought about this question; "what do you mean?"

Katie, "what if he does not like football?"

John, "no son of mine would not like football. He is going to love Manchester United like his old man, and he is going to lead England to a World Cup championship."

Katie, "but, darling, he is only two."

John, "have you seen a two-year old dribble the ball like Josh can?"

Katie, "you can't force him."

John, "I will let him decide. I would never force him."

John started taking Josh to the football fields as soon as he started walking. There John would juggle the ball and show off to his little admirer. Josh learned how to pass and shoot the soccer ball by age two. It is crazy with certain kids. Some kids are just quick learners. Josh was a phenomenal learner. By age three he was able to dribble the football regularly. He was running with the ball like a professional. John knew his little son was gifted. At age three and a half John started taking Josh to Manchester United games. Little Josh was delighted. He was a sponge. He was absorbing football at an extremely fast pace. At age four little Josh had become a regular freak show. John would bring his friends over to his house and ask Josh to juggle the soccer ball four or five times.

John, "little Josh, show your father's friends how you can juggle."

Josh, "no!"

One of John's close friends, James, voiced his opinion, "John, I told you he can't juggle."

John, "do you want to put some money on it, James?"

John's other friend, Robert, joined into the conversation, "of course, my twenty against your five."

John, "no problem."

None of John's friends were aware of the fact that they were getting hustled. This was little Josh's cue. Anytime John's friends would offer money, Josh knew it was time to perform. John and Josh had practiced this scenario hundreds of times.

John, "come on, little buddy, do it for your dad?"

Josh, "no!"

James, "I told you he can't do it."

John, "do you want to raise the stakes, James? My ten against your forty?"

Both Robert and James wanted a piece of this action. With that John smiled at his friends and then told his son to juggle the ball twenty times. Little Josh winked back at his father and started juggling like Pele.

When he got to ten, his father instructed Josh, "only with your head now."

Little Josh kicked his little football higher and started juggling only with his head. When he got to twenty Josh stopped. Neither James nor Robert could believe their eyes. Not only could this four-year old juggle but he could also do it with his head, his thighs, or his feet.

Then all hell broke loose in the house. Robert, amazed, "John, you have something special here."

James, in disbelief, "oh my gosh. We witnessed a miracle."

Robert, shocked, "that is the best forty bucks I have ever spent."

John, "friends, my boy will lead England to a World Cup."

At that moment you could hear a pin drop in the room. There was silence, almost too eerie. Then for the first time in his young life, Josh said something that his father would never forget.

Josh, "I am going to win the World Cup."

John was shocked. He stared at his son for a second and said, "I know, son, you are going to be a great champion like Charlton. Don't you ever forget, your father loves you very much."

CHAPTER 7

❀

Lucky Jack Burns

Robbie Kiel thought about Katie for a long time. He continually replayed that magical night. It was the first time he had ever been with a woman. He wondered to himself on many nights, would I ever see her again? Do I love her? Does she love me? Should I go find her? Should I tell her that I am in love with her? Robbie thought about these questions for a long time. Then he reached a difficult decision. He decided he should not see Katie. Instead he wrote a letter to her and dropped it off at her parent's place. After all, she was a married woman. No matter how much she hated her husband she was still married. Robbie knew leaving her alone was the noble thing to do.

Robbie left Bedlington in the winter of 1981. He had been signed to a minor league contract by a football scout from Manchester United. The scout's name was Jack "Lucky" Burns. He was known around the football circles as Lucky Jack. Lucky Jack had worked for the Manchester United organization for a long time. He had started off as a cleaning boy and moved up through the organization. He was forty-four years old. He had seen the great Bobby Charlton in action at the 1966 World Cup. Lucky Jack had a reputation for discovering talent in unlikely places. He had an unbelievable eye for skill. Lucky Jack had discovered Robbie Kiel while on a scouting trip to watch another prospect from Bedlington. He had never seen Kiel before. As he started watching his prospect, Kiel managed to catch Burns's eye. This Kiel kid did not look like much at first sight. But on this particular day the skinny blonde-headed Englishman was spectacular on that field. Kiel's team had won three to two. Kiel had scored all three of his teams goals. Lucky Jack immediately wanted to know who this kid was. To Lucky Jack it was evident this kid had it all: size, speed, and talent. Kiel was so impressive during the game that Lucky Jack wanted to meet him right away. He thought to himself quietly, how come no one else has ever seen Robbie Kiel? Surely somebody has seen him and signed him to a deal. If not, somebody must have heard about him. There is no way a phenomenal footballer could be going this unnoticed.

After the game Lucky approached Robbie; "Robbie, how would you like to come to Manchester United and train with the big boys?"

Robbie could not believe his ears; "yes, sir, I would love that. Is this a joke? Who are you?"

Lucky Jack replied, "I am a scout for United. People call me Lucky Jack."

Robbie in disbelief, "yes, sir. Nice to meet you, Mr. Lucky Jack."

Lucky Jack smiled, "no, no, Robbie. Just call me Lucky Jack. None of that mister crap."

Kiel, a little embarrassed, "yes, sir."

Jack immediately realized from Kiel's reaction that he was a shy, well-groomed boy, "oh, don't worry, Robbie. Just call me Mr. Lucky Jack. It does not really matter. Whatever you are comfortable with."

Kiel, still a little embarrassed, "yes, sir, Mr. Burns."

Lucky Jack, "look son I want you to come to Manchester with me. I am not promising that you would ever make the A-team but you can train with the B-team until we cut you from the team. You would be getting paid the league minimum. But before I offer you a chance at a contract I must know something. Have you signed with anyone else?"

Robbie, "no, sir."

Lucky Jack was very relieved to hear that Kiel had not been signed by anyone else. He was ecstatic to hear the good news. Lucky Jack decided to check the boy's football knowledge, "who is your favorite player of all time?"

Robbie did not hesitate at all; "Bobby Charlton!"

Lucky Jack was smiling from head to toe. It was as if he had fallen in love again. Charlton was Lucky Jack's hero, too. Lucky Jack was so impressed by the way Kiel handled himself that he wanted to take him to Manchester immediately.

Lucky, "are you ready to come to Manchester with me right now?"

Robbie ecstatic to hear those words, "of course, I would do anything to play for Manchester United. But I don't have any money, and I wouldn't have a place to live in Manchester. I don't know anybody, Mr. Burns. I might even get homesick. I have never left this town before."

Lucky Jack, "don't worry about the minor details. I will take care of everything. I will look after you as if you're my own son until you get cut from the team."

Kiel became aggravated all of the sudden; "if I come to Manchester with you, Mr. Burns, I won't get cut from the team. So you can pretty much forget about that."

With that one statement Lucky Jack knew he had the winning lottery ticket. Not only could this kid play but he had the intangibles other eighteen-year olds did not have. He had heart unlike no other young boy he had ever met. No prospect ever talked to Lucky Jack like that. He had been saying the same thing to prospects for years. This was the first time a prospect had told him to basically shove it up his ass.

Jack changed the subject, "how tall are you?"

Robbie, "six feet two inches."

Jack, "how much do you weigh?"

Robbie, "one hundred and sixty pounds."

Jack, "we have to fill your frame if you ever want to make the A-team."

Robbie, "I will do anything you ask me."

Jack, "how old are you?"

Robbie Kiel, "I just turned nineteen years old."

Jack Burns sat in a bar in Manchester four years after meeting Kiel and was having a conversation with a group of team executives from United. Jack Burns drank his whiskey and told the story of his discovery of young Kiel. People could not believe that no one had ever heard of Kiel until Lucky Jack had come into the picture. The most important one out of all of the guys enjoying Lucky Burns rant and rave was the team owner, Alfred Fredrickson.

Lucky Jack, "what do you think about Robbie Kiel, Mr. Fredrickson?"

Mr. Fredrickson, "I can't believe how you found him. He is just phenomenal. Jack, your reputation proceeds you. Finding talent in unlikely places. You are the best in the business."

Jack, "from day one Robbie's talent was evident, Mr. Fredrickson. He has speed, he has power and he has stamina. But, most of all, he has that intangible Charlton had, he can read the game like no other."

Mr. Fredrickson, "I know, Jack, you have done well."

Lucky Jack, "sir, I would hate to sound conceited but I think I did better than well. Robbie Kiel scored twenty-eight goals in 1982. Last year he scored thirty-three goals, and this year he is already at twenty-five after twenty games. He is going to break every scoring record England has ever seen."

Mr. Fredrickson, "you are right, Lucky Jack. I hope he will be this good in two years to play for us in 1986."

Jack Burns replied with a smile, "World Cup Mexico if he does not get hurt. England will win the cup."

Mr. Fredrickson, smiling also, raised his glass for a toast; "God bless Robbie Kiel, God bless the United and God bless England."

With each goal Robbie Kiel scored his legend grew bigger. In 1985 with one game to go during the regular season Kiel had reached zenith of his young career. Manchester United and Arsenal were tied for first place going into the last game of the season. The winner would go onto claim the league title. The match against Arsenal would be in Old Trafford. The stage was set. It was the Robbie Kiel show from the beginning. Kiel had scored on the fifth minute on a cross with a diving header. The crowd was going crazy. Old Trafford was in frenzy. Kiel struck again in the forty-fifth minute. He received a pass on the eighteen, made one move to his right and then put the ball into the upper ninety with an unbelievable shot. Old Trafford had officially never before been this loud. Manchester United fans were going nuts. At halftime Manchester United was leading Arsenal 2 to 0. In the second half, Manchester United played defense. Manchester had only one player attacking the entire second half, and it was Kiel. In the ninetieth minute Kiel put an end to his show. On a corner kick Kiel one touched a beautiful shot past the out stretched hands of the Arsenal goalie. Manchester United had won the league championship. They had beaten Arsenal 3 to 0. The next morning the papers around England read, "Kiel 3 Arsenal 0." Robbie Kiel had formally arrived onto the football scene of England. Even though he had scored tons of goals before this season, this was the first time he had brought a championship trophy to his beloved United. Every kid in England knew Robbie Kiel's name. Without exception, they all wanted to play football like Robbie Kiel.

After the United versus Arsenal match fans stayed in Old Trafford and chanted, "Robbie! Robbie! Robbie…!" for forty-five minutes. Kiel's name reverberated in Old Trafford. Robbie came out of the locker room with his trademark smile and obliged his worshipers. The entire stadium exploded as if another goal had been scored when they saw Kiel. In the stands that day was a young kid named Josh Roark. He was five years old, and his hero worship had officially begun.

Josh, "Father, do you think I will ever be as good as Robbie Kiel?"

John, to his son, "yes, son. You will be better."

Josh, "do you think that I could meet him?"

John, "one day, son."

Josh, "do you think I could play with him one day?"

John, "if he is still around in fifteen years, why not?"

Josh was extremely bright, "I will be twenty and he will be thirty-eight."

John was impressed by his son's mathematics; "if he is still around by then you can show him some new tricks."

Josh, "Father, can you buy me a number nine Robbie Kiel jersey?"

John lifted his son and put him on his shoulders, "yes, son. Anything for the next Bobby Charlton."

CHAPTER 8

❀

Death

That night when John and his five-year old son Josh returned back to Ashington his mother was waiting for them anxiously. She had heard the news that Manchester United had beaten Arsenal behind her old friend Robbie Kiel's three spectacular goals.

Josh ran inside; "Mommy, Mommy, Father just bought me a Robbie Kiel jersey. I am going to be just like number nine!"

Katie, embracing her son's enthusiasm, "I know, honey, now go inside and wash up. Time for you to go to bed."

Josh, "I am not tired. I want to go outside and play football."

Katie, "time to go to sleep."

Josh did not argue, "okay Mommy, I love you."

Katie was curious about Robbie Kiel so she turned to her husband and asked, "John, how good is Robbie Kiel?"

John was surprised at this question; "honey, you never asked about football before, why are you so curious?"

Katie, "I want to know if he is as good as everybody makes him out to be."

John, "he is the best player to come out of England since Bobby Charlton."

Katie smiled, "okay, honey, I am going to bed. Good night."

John, "good night."

Over the next several years, Josh's infatuation with Robbie Kiel grew. There were at least ten different Robbie Kiel posters in his room. Some posters Josh had Kiel in his United uniform, and some of the other posters had Robbie Kiel in his England national team jersey. Josh wanted to be just like Kiel.

Robbie Kiel had become a household name in England. Not only was Kiel the best player in England, but, also, to many, he was considered to be the best person in England. He was kind, sensitive and generous. Fathers wanted their sons to be like Robbie Kiel, and mothers wanted their daughters to marry a guy like Robbie Kiel. Men wanted to be him, and women wanted to be with him. He was unbelievable. People of England adored Robbie like he was their own son.

In 1990 Josh Roark turned ten years old. Josh's golden locks made him the town sweet heart. He started resembling Kiel so much that people in Ashington started calling little Josh, "little Kiel." Whether it rained or snowed, Josh was outside with his football, constantly playing and wearing his favorite Robbie Kiel jersey. Josh was an unbelievable football phenomenon. There were rumors around Ashington that Lucky Jack had come into town anonymously and watched this young prospect. Everybody in Ashington knew he was going to be the next Robbie Kiel. At ten years old Josh was playing with kids four years older then him. He was still able to dominate these older players. John Roark loved his son and admired him for the person he was becoming. In John's mind, in seven years Josh would be playing for United, and in ten years he would be playing for England. He was so sure of this that he would tell anybody and everybody in Ashington that would listen to him about this fact. Nobody dared to argue with John Roark. They knew little Kiel had the potential to go all the way.

One day in the November winter Josh wanted to go to the football fields and play. But he had no one to play with. It was rainy and cold outside. No parent in their right mind would let their kid go outside in this weather.

Josh, to his father, "Father, let's go play."

John, "Son, it is raining, and it is cold."

Josh turned to his father smartly; "come on, Father, you played in the rain with me before. Let's go play. You know you want to."

John knew that they had played in the rain before as well, "Son, it is raining really hard. Come on, let's play some other night."

Josh insisted, "I bet Robbie Kiel never stopped practicing in the rain."

John, "but, Son, I don't want you to get sick. You have to ask your mother."

Josh knew his mother would never approve of this; "Father, you know mother won't let me."

John, not being able to say no to little Kiel, "I am not going to go play unless it is okay with your mother."

Josh, "okay, Father, I will ask Mother."

John knew Katie would say no, "okay, go ask."

Josh ran into the kitchen, "Mother, can I go outside with Father and play?"

Katie, "not in bloody hell."

Josh, "Mother, please, I have to get better. I want to be like Robbie Kiel."

Katie smiled at her son whom looked more and more like Kiel everyday, "not tonight. It is too cold. You could get sick. Then you won't be able to play for two weeks."

Josh got really angry and threw a temper tantrum; "Mother, you never let me do anything. If it was up to you I would never play football."

Katie did not say anything for a second and then responded sternly, "Josh Roark, go to your room."

Josh crying, "let me play. Let me play please. I want to be like Robbie Kiel. Please let me play. The more I practice, the more I have a chance to meet Robbie Kiel. Please let me play, Mother."

Katie, getting tired of Josh's whining, "I said, no!"

Josh ran into his room. He slammed the door. Katie went after him; "Josh Roark, open your door right this minute."

There was no response. Katie, again yelling at the closed door, "Josh Roark, I will not let you play football for a week if this door is not open by the time I count to five. One, two, three…"

Josh opened his door, "Mother, I want to go play."

Katie stood her ground, "no! Not in weather like this."

During Josh's and Katie's shouting match, John walked in, "Josh, put your boots on. We are going to go play."

Josh, ecstatic to hear this from his father, "yes! Yes! Yes! I love you, Father. You are my hero."

Katie became furious. She turned to her husband; "this is what happens all the time, Josh comes up to me for something, and I say no. Then you know I am against it but you come into the picture like his knight in shining armor and save him. You make me look like the bad guy."

John, "honey, he is just a kid."

Katie, yelling at John, "no, he is not just a kid. He is a spoiled brat. You give him everything he wants. You give and then give him some more. You need to quit spoiling him."

John was still calm, "honey, he is just a kid. I only have one son."

Katie, "why must you undermine my authority? Why do you do this to me?"

John, "I am not undermining your authority. I am not doing anything to you. All we want to do is go play."

Katie, angrier with John more then ever now, "you just don't understand, do you? Do you think I am stupid? Do you think I don't see what you are doing?"

John, "no! I don't think you are stupid. I am not doing anything, honey."

Katie started running to her room, crying and yelling, "I hate you, John."

John was angry now, also, "I hate you, too."

John turned to his son, "let's go play, Josh."

Josh was shaken up seeing his mother crying for the first time, "I don't want to play anymore, Father."

John raised his voice, "put your clothes on, now."

Josh simply did what he was told, "okay, Father."

With that one powerful order, father and son had left their house to go play in the rain. Meanwhile Katie cried herself to sleep. They had been gone for almost an hour. Josh was having a great time running around in the muddy field with his father. Josh had forgotten a fight even had happened at home.

Josh, "let's play a match, Father. First one to three wins."

John, "okay. But then we have to go home before we get sick."

Josh, "okay, Father."

John, "the loser has to do dishes for the next month."

Josh, laughing in the rain, "okay, Father."

Their game of one-on-one had begun. Josh went around his father with a couple of nice moves and scored the first goal, 1-0.

Josh, taunting his father, "come on, Father, you can do better."

John was not taking it easy on his son at all. He had always tried to instill in his son the power of competition. Plus, John Roark was an excellent football player himself. Rumors around Ashington were that when John Roark was a young man he had been scouted by Lucky Burns. Lucky Burns had invited John Roark to try out for the United but Roark never had enough courage to go try out. That was John's biggest regret in life. He wanted his son to have what he could not accomplish.

John made a nice move to his left using his bigger body to shield little Josh and then went around Josh to score. The match was tied at one a piece.

John, smiling and taunting his boy, "come on, my little buddy. Robbie Kiel would not let me do that to him."

Josh replied angrily, "I will show you, Father."

Josh took the ball and started dribbling straight at his father as fast as he could. John was watching his son in admiration while backpedaling to his goal. During his dribble, Josh had picked up a move where, when he got closer to his father, he would throw his left foot over the ball as fast as he could and go to his right. Little Kiel had become so good that he could do this move with either foot and go in either direction. John had slowed down backpedaling and marveled at this magnificent move. As he watched little Kiel, John felt as if he was watching the move in slow motion, over and over in his head. When Josh had finished the move, John had been burned. Little Kiel had scored. He was ahead two to one.

Josh, smiling more now, "come on, Father!"

John was drenched in pouring rain and did not look good at all. He pulled his son aside in the monsoon and told him, "no matter what happens, I love you, son. Let's go home now."

Josh, "I love you, too, Father. Let me go pick up the ball."

Josh ran to get his favorite ball in the rain. When he turned around his father was laying face first in the rain.

Josh ran, screaming as loudly as he could towards his father, "Father, Father, what is wrong? What did I do wrong?"

John Roark did not respond.

Josh, screaming really loudly, "somebody help me! My father is hurt! Help me! Help me!"

There was no response from the darkness.

Josh cried as he held his father's head, "Father, please wake up, please wake up, please wake up. I love you. I love you, Father, you are my hero. Please wake up. I did not mean to hurt you. I will never make that stupid move again. I am ready to go home. Please wake up. Please wake up. I promise I will never want to play in the rain again."

John Roark would never see the daylight again. He had passed away from a heart attack on that rainy November night in 1990. He was forty-five years old.

CHAPTER 9

Buxton Life Insurance

It had been two weeks since John Roark's passing. John's death surprised many people. John's parents, Larry and Elizabeth Roark, were distraught. They were the same age as Katie's parents, Henry and Mary Owen. Their son's passing hurt them tremendously. They were really close to their son and their grandson. Since they lived in Ashington John would bring little Josh to his parent's house every chance he had. Of course, that would be almost everyday.

Larry turned to Katie after the funeral and said, "I should have died before my son. He had the rest of his life ahead of him. He needed to see his boy grow up. He needed to see his son get married. But he didn't. I should have died before him."

Katie hugged her father-in-law, "I love you, Dad. Everything is going to be okay."

Elizabeth, holding little Josh, "Katie, we have to talk to you about something."

Katie did not pay attention to Elizabeth at all, "okay, Mother. We will talk later."

John's passing especially hurt his father. Larry knew John had many plans with his son. John had figured out the rest of Josh's life. Now he would not have the chance to witness his son's greatness. This fact alone really ate away at Larry. Larry Roark knew little Josh was destined for greatness. As he thought about these things, suddenly, from the corner of his eye, he caught little Josh hiding under the dinner table. Larry smiled at his grandson and motioned to little Josh to come out. Little Josh saw his grandfather's gesture and ignored him. Larry thought for a second, why won't that boy come next to me? In the past, little Josh would do anything to be around his grandfather.

Larry approached the table and leaned down underneath it, "little Josh, come out, and talk with me."

Little Josh, "no, Grandfather. I don't want to talk."

Larry, "come on, buddy, let's talk."

Little Josh looked at his grandfather and asked, "when is Father going to wake up?"

Larry was torn inside with this question, he did not know what to say so he changed the subject; "how about that Robbie Kiel scoring four goals against Turkey?"

Little Josh, "I don't care about Robbie Kiel, Grandfather. I don't care about football. I want to know when my father is going to wake up."

Larry knelt under the table and sat next to his grandson, "look, Josh, I love you. Your grandmother loves you. Your mother loves you. Your grandfather, Henry, and your grandmother, Mary, loves you. Your father will always love you. But he is not going to wake up, son. He is dead, and he went to heaven."

Josh started screaming at Larry, "I want my father. He is not dead. He is alive."

Larry tried to catch the boy as he ran out from under the table; "Josh, wait a second now."

Katie ran towards the table and asked, "what happened?"

Larry, with tears in his eyes, "nothing! Little Josh wants his father back."

It had been a month since John Roark's passing. Out of all the people in Ashington, naturally Katie had taken her husband's death the hardest. She felt guilty that he died so young. She had thought to herself many nights, if I did not fight with him that night, maybe he would not have died. Part of her blamed herself. She thought, maybe I could have been more truthful with him over the years. I could have told him years earlier that Josh was not his son. But she thought about telling him the truth many times. But how would a recovering alcoholic take something like that? Would he have started drinking again? Would he have beaten on Katie for sleeping around? Surely so! Josh was John's night and day. He had given up his biggest love of alcohol for his son.

John's death left Katie with troubles she had not worried about ever before. Even though they did not have any bills, and the house was paid for, she had to get a job and put little Josh through college. Katie was lost for words. Many nights she would drink liquor and cry herself to sleep. Her main question during these drinking binges was what am I going to do?

A month after John's death, a couple of guys showed up at Katie's doorstep.

Katie looked at these guys with black suits; "can I help you?"

The taller gentleman responded, "are you Katie Roark?"

Katie, looking a little confused, "yes, I am. May I ask who is asking?"

The taller gentleman responded again, "yes, my name is Shadrick Stennis with Buxton Life Insurance."

Katie, "yes, I have heard of Buxton Life Insurance. Only if you could have been here several years ago, then you could have helped me. Needless to say, I am not buying what you are selling."

Insurance agent Stennis smiled and said, "we are not selling anything, Mrs. Roark."

Katie looked at him with aggravation, "forgive me for being rude, but if you are not selling anything, then why the hell are you here?"

Mr. Stennis, "can I come in?"

Katie hesitant but stern, "no, you may not."

Mr. Stennis, understanding her refusal to let him in, "I am here to settle your husband's life insurance policy, Mrs. Roark."

Katie, dumbfounded, "my husband never had any insurance. Is this some kind of freaking joke?"

Mr. Stennis, serious as he could be, "no, ma'am, this is not a joke. And, yes, Mrs. Roark, your husband did have life insurance. On October 12,

1980, he came to Buxton Life Insurance with his father, Mr. Larry Roark, and purchased for himself life insurance worth $250,000."

Katie, still looking puzzled, "no, that can't be. My deceased husband was not that bright."

Mr. Stennis, apparently understanding the sensitivity of the situation, softened his voice, "I want you to look at this signature, is this John Roark's signature?"

Katie looked at the signature, she could not believe her eyes; "it sure is."

Mr. Stennis, "can I come in now?"

Katie, looking more confused then ever, "sure! Come on in. I am sorry for being so rude earlier. I have a lot of pressure on me."

Mr. Stennis smiled, "no problem. I understand the stress that you must be going through."

Katie, "thank you for being so understanding."

Mr. Stennis, "we have all the proper paperwork. We know John Roark had died of natural causes. Therefore, you are entitled to receive this money from us. On his policy, he had stated that you, his wife, Katie Roark, are the primary benefactor of all the money in case of his death."

Katie, "how did you know he passed away?"

Mr. Stennis, "Mr. Larry Roark informed us about three weeks ago."

Katie thought for a second, I guess that is what they had been trying to tell me for a month now. Katie, thinking aloud, "I guess I should not have ignored them. But I wanted the pain to go away."

Mr. Stennis, "what was that?"

Katie smiled; "nothing. I am thinking out loud."

Katie was getting emotional; "why am I the primary benefactor of this policy?"

Mr. Stennis replied, "I don't know, Mrs. Roark. But here is your name on the policy as the primary benefactor. Your husband wanted all the money to go to you."

Katie had all kinds of questions to ask, "why me?"

Mr. Stennis, "I guess because you are his wife."

Katie did not know what to say, "me!"

Mr. Stennis ignored her for a second; "Buxton Life Insurance will give you a cashiers check for $250,000 once we complete all the paperwork. This process will take up to ten to twelve working days."

Katie, puzzled, but held her emotions in check, "what do you need me to do?"

Mr. Stennis, "you have to sign this line acknowledging that you will be receiving this payment."

Katie, "sure." And then signed the insurance papers.

Mr. Stennis, "I am all done here. Thank you for your time."

Katie, looking as if she had the whole world lifted off her shoulders, "no, Mr. Stennis, thank you. Again, I am sorry for being so rude earlier."

After the meeting with the Buxton Insurance men Katie was all alone in her house. Little Josh had went to school two hours earlier. Katie had many questions that needed to be answered, October 12, 1980? That was the day after little Josh was born. Katie now remembered how, that morning John had left the hospital without saying anything to anybody and was gone for hours with his father. When he had left, Katie thought to herself, old fool went to get plastered in his moment of happiness. But, now, Katie felt bad for how she thought about her husband on that day. She had millions of questions to ask John but he was gone now. A little too late Katie sure did not want to ask her father-in-law Larry Roark any questions about this matter. She could not stand how torn they were. Being around Larry and Elizabeth only made Katie want to slit her own throat.

It was clear that Katie could not ask John anymore questions since he was dead. She did what he would do if he were in her situation. She picked up a bottle of Jack Daniels, drank it and then asked the empty house in a drunken rage, "did I know John Roark at all?" Katie responded to her question more loudly and with anger, "apparently not! Even though I was with him for fourteen years I never guessed he would do something this responsible." Katie again asked her empty house another question, "what kind of man would be prepared for something like this?" She responded to her question with a lot of sarcasm, "of course, a very intelligent man." Katie, screaming louder, asked again to the empty house, "was he not as bad as I thought?" Katie, crying now, answered her own question, "I guess not! I guess not!"

Katie, yelling even louder now, "did he really love me?"

Quietly she answered to herself, "maybe."

Katie was crying so loudly now that the neighbors could hear her. She asked as loudly as she could to an empty house, "did he know Josh was not his?"

Katie responded to her question laying on the floor in an incoherent state, "I don't think so."

She asked many other questions that day alone in the house. One of the questions that puzzled her most was, "if John knew Josh was not his, how could he hide something of that magnitude from me?" With that last question Katie Roark passed out into oblivion.

CHAPTER 10

❀

1986 Mexico

Robbie Kiel played in his first World Cup in1986 in Mexico. Robbie had become one of the brightest stars of the World Cup. However, there was another superstar whose light shone a little bit brighter than Kiel's that year. That shinier star belonged to the Argentine international, Diego Maradona.

World Cup 1986 in Mexico started very fast for young Robbie. Since this was his first World Cup, he was extremely anxious to play. In previous years, he had done really well with the United. He had been selected as the European Footballer of the Year in 1985, and all eyes were on him in Mexico. On June 3, 1986, Kiel made his debut appearance for England in Mexico. England's first opponent was Portugal. Before the game started, Kiel thought he was going to pass out. He was having an anxiety attack. He had thrown up a couple of times all the way to the starting whistle. But once the whistle blew, he was all right. He no longer felt sick. On this day, England would be plagued by missed opportunities. In the tenth minute, Kiel had a real chance to score. He was one-on-one with the Portugal goalkeeper, he shot the ball and the ball ricocheted off of the goalkeeper, then hit the right goal post and went out of bounds. Kiel knew he should have scored. He had never missed a one-on-one before. But this was just one example of many missed English chances throughout the game. Portugal had one chance early on, and they capitalized on it. In the end, Kiel had lost his World Cup debut to Portugal 1-0.

Fans of England were heart broken. They knew for the rest of the cup they could not afford anymore defeats. One more defeat and England was out of Mexico. England's second game was three days later against Morocco. They knew the stakes were high. But this time, Kiel was ready. He did not have any butterflies in his stomach before the Morocco match. The Morocco game was the continuation of the Portugal game. England had many chances, and, again they could not take advantage of them. In the seventeenth minute, Kiel had taken a shot from outside the eighteen that hit the crossbar. Fifty-three minutes later, in the seventieth minute on a corner kick, Kiel headed another ball to the crossbar. The match ended up tied at zero.

While the English fans in Mexico were very well behaved, the English papers were going crazy back at home. Before England's third game in the World Cup, one of London's most prestigious newspapers wrote, "If England Loses Apocalypse Is Upon Us." Going into the third game of the group stage, England's group was very crowded at the top. England had one draw and one defeat. Morocco had one win and two draws. This meant that Morocco would advance for sure. Portugal had one win and two loses. Everything came down to England versus Poland. Poland had one win and a draw. All they had to do was tie or beat England and Poland would advance to the second round.

England's game versus Poland was on June 11, 1986. The day before the game, the English newspapers interviewed their superstar, Kiel. One sports columnist who had been following Kiel since day one was William Thacker. Over the past four years Thacker and Kiel had become friends. Kiel understood Thacker's job and respected him, whether Thacker wrote a good story about him or not. At the same time, Thacker respected Kiel as a phenomenon and as a gentleman. Thacker was in his early fifties, but he knew he had only seen two other gentlemen that were better at their sport. Of course, they were Bobby Charlton and Bobby Moore.

Mr. Thacker, during the interview with Kiel, "Robbie, what is wrong with England?"

Kiel, "Mr. Thacker, nothing really. We have been unlucky."

Mr. Thacker, "you led our league in goals. Why can't you score here?"

Kiel was aggravated by this question, but still the gentlemen, he answered, "I have been unlucky, sir."

Mr. Thacker, realizing his friend's uneasiness, pressed on, "to what do you attribute your team's unluckiness?"

Kiel smiled and responded, "not being able to score goals."

Mr. Thacker, "you know, Robbie, you have to beat Poland by a couple of goals in order to have the tie break over them."

Kiel, "I am aware of that."

Mr. Thacker, "how do you expect to score?"

Kiel was really aggravated now; "look, we will score, and we will win big. Matter of fact, I will score. You worry about selling your stupid newspaper, and let me worry about advancing to the second round."

Mr. Thacker was shocked. He had never seen Kiel this angry, "I am sorry, Robbie, if I angered you. I am just doing my job."

Kiel became angrier, "I know you are doing your job. But all you want is a headline."

Mr. Thacker was a little embarrassed; "you know I do, Robbie."

Kiel, even more frustrated got up; "here is a headline for you, Mr. Thacker, Kiel guarantees that he will score three goals against Poland. No more questions, this interview is officially over. I will score three against Poland. Write that down and take a picture."

On June 11, 1986, headlines in England read, "Kiel Guarantees Three Goals Against Poland." It was time for the game. Before the game started, it was evident during the referee and captain meetings that the Poland Internationals were upset by Kiel's comments. Once the game began, it had became clear Kiel had angered the Polish national team. Every time Kiel touched the ball during the first five minutes of the game he was getting fouled. Not only was Kiel getting fouled but he was getting fouled hard. This fueled the English superstar. Kiel started playing on pure adrenaline. In the twenty-fifth minute, Kiel struck. He got the ball thirty-five yards from Poland's goal, went around four players and suddenly he was one-on-one with the Polish goalie. The goalie came out of the goal and dove to Kiel's feet. As the goalie dove Kiel softly chipped the ball over the goalie and put England up one to nothing.

Kiel was not going to let England get eliminated on this day or on any other day. He knew one goal was not enough. In the forty-ninth minute, Kiel scored on a free kick. A minute earlier, Kiel was fouled hard by the Polish defender outside the Poland box. The referee had given a yellow card for that foul. However, Kiel was not satisfied with the yellow, he got up and argued with the referee. He started letting the referee know that foul deserved a red card.

Kiel, yelling, "sir, that foul was intentional. He tried to injure me."

The referee replied, "Robbie, you are getting a fair shake."

Meanwhile, as Kiel complained, a skirmish had broken out between the two teams. Kiel's teammates had come to their captain's rescue. Poland set up their wall with directions from their goalie. It was a five-man wall. Kiel looked at the wall, then looked at the goalkeeper and hit a bullet to the right of the wall. The ball found the lower corner of the Polish net, and England had gone up two to nothing behind Kiel's spectacular free kick. Kiel's killer instinct had taken over. He was like a shark in water that had smelled blood. This is why he was selected a year earlier as the European Footballer of The Year. These were the reasons he had won Europe's most prestige award, the Golden Boot. Kiel was playing a different kind of game than the rest of his teammates and the Polish national team. In the seventy-eighth minute, Kiel scored again. This time it was on a simple corner kick. His teammate had sent a gorgeous high cross, but Kiel was the only one who had jumped high enough to connect to the ball with his head. The ball went to the left side of the goalie where he stood motionless. England three, Poland nothing. After scoring his third goal of the game, Kiel ran towards his bench and pointed at his heart. England had won the game. They would advance to the second round.

The next morning, English newspapers read, "Messiah Delivers On His Promise." Kiel's fame had grown over night. No footballer had ever made a prediction this big on the world's biggest stage and backed up his prediction like Kiel had. He had told the world how many he was going to score, and then he went out there and did what he had said he would do. In England and around the world, people looked at Kiel as a gift from the football gods.

A week after Kiel's guarantee, England would face Paraguay. Paraguay had an exceptional team. However, again England was that much better on this day. As soon as the whistle blew, Kiel's teammates started playing inspired football. By the fifteenth minute, England had gone up one to zero on Kiel's penalty kick. In the fifty-third minute, England struck again making the score two to nothing. Kiel and England had one more left in them. Kiel received a soft pass outside the eighteen yard line and made one quick move to his left to shake off the defender, and then Kiel took a shot that sailed over the goalie's head to the back of the net. England three, Paraguay nothing.

England had advanced to the quarter finals. Great Britain now was in a frenzy. Robbie Kiel had official became the leading goal scorer in World Cup 1986 with five goals. England's next opponent would be the South American powerhouse, Argentina, led by their superstar, Diego Maradona. On June 22, 1986, the game of the decade was about to be on the way. English papers had dubbed this game as, "Maradona Versus Kiel. Game For Football Supremacy." On this particular day, Argentina was just a tad better then England. They had won a close contest with two goals from Maradona. Kiel was able to score one to tie the score at one. However, Maradona scored on a goal that the whole world saw as a handball. Everyone saw the handball except the referees. With that goal, England's World Cup hopes came to an end. Once the whistle blew to end the match, Kiel fell to his knees in the middle of the field and cried like a little kid. His coaches and his teammates tried to console him, but he could not stop sobbing. Kiel knew he would have to wait four more years at a chance to win the World Cup. Later on, tabloids dubbed Maradona's goal as, "Hand of God." After the defeat against Argentina, Great Britain was devastated. The next day in England, the picture Kiel crying in the middle of the field with his hands on his knees was on the cover of every newspaper in the British Kingdom, and the cover read, "Fallen Hero!" A week later, Argentina knocked off West Germany to win World Cup Mexico. Argentina winning the cup was a salt in England's open wound. The people of England hated the fact that Argentina won the cup.

After the World Cup, Kiel returned back to England with his team. He was still devastated by England's defeat. His status as an English football icon had reached to new heights. English fans loved Kiel more than ever now. England had never witnessed an athlete showing his emotions like Kiel had. They respected him for it. England felt like they knew him more now. He was no longer the young phenomenon in the English fans' eyes, but now England looked at him as they looked at their favorite son, Bobby Charlton. Robbie Kiel had become a true English football legend in five short years.

CHAPTER 11

❀

Hating Football

It was 1991. It had been a year since John Roark had passed away. His son, the future football star, had become incredibly quiet. All Josh would ever do after his father's death was lock himself in his room and read American books. American football and the American culture had fascinated Josh since his father died. Even though he was very intelligent, Josh Roark started getting bad grades in school. Josh went from a very gregarious person to an outsider in the past year. He had taken all of his football posters out of his room and put them away permanently. Even worse, he had not played football ever since his father's death.

Katie, "Josh, tell me what is wrong."

Josh, looking at an empty space, "nothing, Mother."

Katie, "you know, I love you, don't you?"

Josh, "I know, Mother, I love you, too."

Katie, "tell me what is wrong."

Josh just stared at her, "nothing, Mother."

Katie, "you never got bad grades. Is everything okay in school?"

Josh, staring at her, "Mother, I don't want to go to school anymore."

Katie, "but you used to love your school. Why don't you want to go all of a sudden?"

Josh, "I don't know!"

Katie, "is somebody picking on you in school?"

Josh, "no, Mother, nobody is picking on me. I just hate Ashington."

Katie, "you never hated Ashington before."

Josh angry now, "I hate Ashington now."

Katie, trying to find a solution, "do you want to go to Bedlington?"

Josh angrier, "I hate Bedlington, too."

Katie, trying to figure out what Josh wanted, "but why?"

Josh started screaming at Katie; "I don't know why! Stop asking me these stupid questions!"

Katie tried to change the subject; "why did you take all of your posters down?"

Josh, "I don't like football anymore."

Katie felt very hurt at this statement, "but, Josh, that is what you wanted to do."

Josh, "I hate football."

Katie started feeling horrible, "why don't you go outside and try to play?"

Josh responded quickly, "no! I am done with football."

Katie, "then what do you want to do?"

Josh did not have a clue, he shrugged his shoulders and said, "I don't know."

Before Josh was born, Katie had wished on many occasions that her husband would drink himself to death and die. But those wishes had never come true. Even after Josh was born Katie thought John would never last without drinking. However, John Roark, the stubborn bastard that he was, had proven her wrong once again. John Roark never had a drink again until he died. Katie had actually grown to liking John since he had quit drinking. She respected him as a father. She even thought that he was an excellent father. She had also learned to respect John as a person. She thought to herself many nights, who could push away their sickness in order to become a role model to his son? She could not think of many people, but her husband was one of those people that would drop everything important in his life for his son.

Josh started getting in more trouble at school. One Tuesday afternoon Katie had been called to school. Josh had gotten into a fight. He had broken a kid's nose for no good reason. Katie came to school and picked up her son. On the ride home Katie wanted to know why.

Katie, "Josh, tell me what you want to do."

Josh had a black eye; "nothing."

Katie, "what do you mean, nothing?"

Josh, looking like a raccoon, "nothing, Mother. I don't want to do anything."

Katie, "I am taking you to your grandparents."

Josh, "no, I am not going. I told you, I hate Bedlington."

Katie, "well, why?"

Josh, crying quietly now, "because Bedlington is Robbie Kiel's town. Every time I think about Robbie Kiel and Bedlington I think about Father."

Katie had not seen Josh cry since the funeral, "it is okay to miss your father. I miss him, too."

Josh, still crying quietly, "you know why I hate Ashington?"

Katie, not knowing what to say, "no. Why?"

Josh, crying a little bit more now, "because this is Bobby Charlton's town. He is my father's hero. All the good things that ever happened to me happened here. I miss Father every time I go to school. I miss him every time I hear Charlton's name. I miss him every time I walk by his bar. I miss him, Mother. I miss him when I see his friends."

Katie, crying with Josh now, "it is okay to miss him, son. I miss him, too."

Josh began to cry more loudly, "Mother, I want to leave England. I want to leave and go somewhere no one knows me. I want to go somewhere no one knows Bobby Charlton or Robbie Kiel."

Katie, hugging her son tightly and crying with him, "where do you want to go, son? Tell me where. I will take you there."

Josh could not stop crying; his bruised eyes and cheeks were full of tears, "I want to go where Huckleberry Finn's adventures happened."

Katie, holding her son tighter, "where?"

Josh, crying, "I want to go to America, Mother."

Katie, in disbelief holding onto Josh, "you want to go to America?"

Josh, still crying, "Mother, if I did not beg Father to play that night he would still be alive. It is my fault that he is dead."

Katie held Josh even tighter and said, "listen to me, little Josh, it is not your fault that your father died that night. People just die. It was his turn to go to heaven."

Josh hugged his mother tightly; "do you believe in heaven, Mother?"

Katie, still crying, "yes, Josh, I do. As we speak, your father is in heaven watching us."

Josh calmed down a little bit; "Mother, you know what he said to me before he died?"

Katie's tears were rolling down her red cheeks; "no. What?"

Josh's big swollen eyes opened wide; "he told me no matter what happens that he loves me."

Katie smiled, "he still loves you, son. He still does. I love you, too."

Josh smiled back at his mother, wiped his tears away and said, "let's go to America, Mother."

Katie did not hesitate a second on that November day; "okay, I will take us to America. But you have to promise me something."

Josh, wiping his tears, "what, Mother?"

Katie, "we will go to America in June. That is eight months from now. I need you to not get in anymore trouble in school. I also need good grades from you. Can you do that for me?"

Josh did not waste a second; "okay, Mother. I will get good grades, and I won't get in anymore trouble."

CHAPTER 12

❀

Oregon

In the spring of 1992, Josh was out of school for spring break. He had been doing well again in school. He started getting back to his old routine. In the past he would go to school and play football. Now he would go to school, and then after school he would go running for hours. After he finished running he would take a shower and then lock himself in his room. His room was no longer a shrine to English football. Now his walls were full of American posters. He had posters of the Grand Canyon, the Empire State Building, Hollywood, Magic Johnson and Michael Jordan. Josh was ready to move to America. Two more months were left before he and his mother were to move. On this particular Friday afternoon, Josh came out of his room and went to find his mother in the house.

Josh, "Mother?"

Katie, "yes, Son, I am in the living room."

Josh, "Mother, I know we are moving soon, but we have not discussed what city in America we are going to."

Katie, "Josh, I don't have any preference, do you?"

Josh, "no, Mother, but I would like to move somewhere that we would both like."

Katie hugged her son and said, "that is very thoughtful."

Josh, "how about I bring the United States map from my room and we pick ourselves a destination."

Katie did not want to disappoint her son. This was the first time in a year and half Josh had come out of his room early like this. Katie said, "sure, go get the map, my king."

Josh smiled and went to his room. A couple of minutes later, he was back with a giant United States Map.

Josh, "where should I put the map?"

Katie pointed at the floor, "right here in the middle of the room, my king."

Josh was having a blast at the fact that his mother was calling him her king. Josh, "how about New York?"

Katie, "no, New York is too crowded."

Josh, "how about Chicago?"

Katie, "nah, too many Irish."

Josh, "how about Boston?"

Katie, "too much politics."

Josh was surprised at his mother's answers, "how about Maine?"

Katie, "no, I would like to go somewhere a little different"

Josh, "Mother, how about Mississippi?"

Katie, "no! That is a little too different."

Josh, "but, Mother, Huck Finn had his great adventures there."

Katie, "Josh, don't you want to be different? Why would you go somewhere that people had already written stories about? Don't you want to create your own stories?"

Josh understood his mother's logic. Josh, "you are right, Mother."

Katie, "how about Indiana?"

Josh, "no! It sounds too much like India."

Katie smiled, "how about Wisconsin?"

Josh, "no, Mother, it is too cold there. I also read in my books that the only things people do in Wisconsin is eat cheese and get drunk. It is the cheese capital of the world."

Katie, "I am sorry, my king. I forgot you don't like cheese. How about Idaho?"

Josh, with a smile, "Mother, do you really want to live somewhere with a goofy name like that?"

Katie was laughing now, she could not remember the last time she had this much fun with her little boy; "yes, my king, you are right."

Now they were both laughing. Josh, "how about Washington?"

Katie, "nah, if I wanted to live in the capital, I would like to live in London."

Josh, "me, too."

Katie, trying to sneak one past Josh, "how about London?"

Josh, "no, Mother, I want to live in America."

Katie smiled at her king; "how about Texas?"

Josh, "I don't think so! Too many cowboys."

Katie was truly enjoying this; she thought they might have a better life in America. Just talking about America had gotten Josh out of his shell. She thought to herself silently, if we lived there, then our relationship would be back to normal.

Katie, "how about California?"

Josh, "I don't know, Mother. California is big. What about you?"

Katie, "California does not sound that bad."

Josh, "okay, we will put California on this side, as a maybe."

Katie, "that sounds good to me."

Josh, "how about Florida?"

Katie, "too close to Cuba."

Josh, "so?"

Katie, with a smile, "if there is a war between Cuba and the U.S., Florida would be the first target."

Josh, "okay, then I will say no to Florida. How about Nevada?"

Katie, "too hot. But we could always live in Las Vegas."

Josh, a little hesitant, "too many lights, Mother."

Katie, "how about Oregon?"

Josh, silent for a second, "I don't know anything about Oregon. But how about you, Mother?"

Katie had apparently anticipated this discussion and done her homework as well; "I like Oregon. It is like here. It rains there all the time. Plus Portland is their biggest city. It is really pretty there and is close to Washington, California and Nevada."

Josh thought about it for a second and then asked, "do you want to live in Oregon, Mother?"

Katie, "sure, I would like that. But since this is your idea to move to America, it is your decision where we live."

Josh, jumping up and down, like a typical eleven and a half-year-old boy would, "I am fine with Oregon. I love you, Mother. Let's go to Oregon."

Katie hugged her little king and became very excited about going to Oregon. But most of all, Katie was excited about having a fresh start with her son. This was the most she had spoken to him in almost a year and a half. She knew there was hope. She also knew Josh would be okay now.

Katie turned to Josh; "I want to go see my parents in Bedlington this weekend. Would you like to go?"

Josh shrugged his shoulders; "Mother, can I just stay here with grandfather Larry and grandmother Elizabeth?"

Katie, "if that is what you want."

Josh, "yes, Mother, I would like to stay here in Ashington."

Katie, "okay, my king. I will let Larry and Elizabeth know that you are staying with them for a few days."

Josh, "thanks, Mother."

On her trip to Bedlington, Katie had many things going on in her head. She thought about her little king back in Ashington. She was so happy that he was finally coming out of his shell. It had been too long since she could remember Josh being excited about anything. She also thought a lot about the America idea and thought it was brilliant. She was thirty-seven years old now, and she needed a fresh start just like Josh. She had not told her parents about the trip to America, but it was time. She would let them know this weekend. Katie was not sure how her parents would take the news.

It had been twelve years since Katie had been in Bedlington. During the past several years, her parents would come to visit her, John and Josh. Her mother was puzzled by the fact that Katie never wanted to come back home to Bedlington. When Katie was young, she would always want to be in Bedlington every chance she had. But after little Josh was born, Katie had become a different person.

> Her mother always asked Katie the same question on every one of her visits to Ashington; "why don't you bring little Josh to us? Come stay with us for a week."

> Katie would always respond the same way; "I don't know mother. It is easier this way."

> Mary would just look at her and then say, "whatever you say, sweetheart."

Katie wanted to tell her mother the truth for years. But it was too hard. How would her mother and father take to the idea that their daughter was a whore? Katie thought about it and then decided it was best if I don't say anything at all. Katie's parents were deeply religious people. Katie knew in her heart if she had told them about Robbie Kiel, they would probably never speak to her again.

CHAPTER 13

❀

Seeing Robbie

Katie made it to Bedlington and her parents' home on a Saturday afternoon. Her plans were to stay in Bedlington that Saturday night and return back home to Ashington the next night. She had made up her mind to let her parents know about her plans to move to America. Her parents were very happy to see their daughter finally visiting them after twelve long years.

Henry, jokingly with a silly grin on his face, "I am surprised you found your way back home."

Katie, smiling back, "Father, you know I had my reasons."

Mary, "where is my little grandson?"

Katie, "he wanted to stay back in Ashington."

Mary, saddened, "he hasn't been here more than two times in his entire life. Don't you think it would have been nice for him to visit?"

Katie, "yeah, it could have been nice. But he wanted to stay back at home."

Henry, "you should have brought him, Katie. I could have taken him to where Robbie Kiel grew up. I am pretty sure he would have been delighted."

Mary, "it is okay you didn't bring little Josh. I have been meaning to ask you, sweetheart, for a long time; what is your reason for not coming home? What reasons kept you away from home all these years?"

Katie did not want to answer her questions; "I came here for a different reason, Mother."

Henry, "what reason is that?"

Mary, "yes, what is your reason now?"

Henry, "do you need money?"

Katie, "no, Father."

Mary, "are you sick?"

Katie, "no, Mother."

Mary, "is Josh sick?"

Katie, "no, Mother."

Henry was dying from the suspense; "let me get this straight; you don't need money from us. You and your son are healthy."

Katie, smiling once again, "yes, Father you are right."

Mary, "then what is your big reason?"

Katie, a little hesitant, "I am taking Josh to America this summer. It is a permanent move."

Mary's jaw dropped; "what are you talking about? Why would you want to do that?"

Henry, puzzled, "Katie, what the hell is wrong with you? Why would you leave your loved ones and go to America?"

Katie, "Josh and I need a change."

Mary, angry at Katie's comment, "Katie, you are still that same dumb kid you were twenty years ago. You never grew up. Why are you so irresponsible? If you need change go to London, go somewhere else. Don't take our only grandson away from us all the way to America."

Henry, furious as well, "I won't let you go to America. What the hell is wrong with you?!"

Katie, "there is nothing wrong with me. It was my son's decision."

Henry, even more furious, "you are going to let an eleven-year old decide? What kind of mother are you?!"

Mary, "Katie, you can't run from your problems. Stay here, and we will help you get through them as a family. Don't run from the life you know."

Henry, agreeing with his wife, "your mother is right. The last twelve years you ran from your problems. Why didn't you come here to visit us one time?"

Katie, "I am not running from my problems. We just need a fresh start."

Mary, "you are running. If you were not running you would not leave this country."

Katie, "do you have any idea how hard it is to raise a little boy by yourself?"

Mary, "I raised you, didn't I?"

Katie, "do you know, ever since John's death, he locks himself in his room for hours and does not come out?"

Mary, saddened by the news, "no! But that is still not a good reason to leave behind everything you know."

Henry, again agreeing with his wife, "yes, your mother is right, Katie. Josh will get over his father's death with time."

Katie, "you know what my son told me the other day? He blamed himself for his father's death. He blamed himself so much that he quit playing the only thing that he ever loved doing. Did you know Josh took down all his posters? Yes, he did, no more Kiel, no more Charlton and sure as hell no more English football posters."

Henry, "why did he do that?"

Mary, "yes, why did he do that?"

Katie, "because everything he knows here reminds him of his father. In Ashington, all he could think about are his football days with his father. He wants to leave Ashington because it is Charlton's birthplace. Charlton was John's hero."

Henry, with a questioned look, "little Josh said that?"

Katie, "yes. It is amazing, huh?"

Henry, "I can't believe how deeply that little boy thinks. Why don't you move to Bedlington?"

Mary, "yes, honey, move here."

Katie, "I will tell you why. Because this is Robbie Kiel's town, Josh worships Robbie Kiel no more. He hates Bedlington because it reminds him of his father. It reminds him of all the football games he went to go see with his father."

Mary, "but how?"

Katie, frustrated, "do I have to spell everything out to you?! Robbie Kiel was his favorite hero. John took Josh to watch Kiel play at a young age. Every time the boy thinks of Bedlington, he thinks of Kiel. Then he thinks about his deceased father."

Henry, "he actually said that?"

Katie, with sarcasm, "no, Father, I am just making things up as I go. I have a great imagination."

Mary, more compassionate now, "but, honey, even if you leave England, all of the things that you are running from will still be here. Ashington, Bedlington, Robbie Kiel and, of course, Bobby Charlton. Do you honestly think nobody knows who those two people are in America?"

Katie, with a big smile, "I know all those things will still be here. But in Josh's mind, he will be leaving all those things behind. Mother, I don't think anybody knows who Kiel and Charlton are in America. Even if they did, only a handful of people do."

Henry knew Katie had made up her mind, and this angered him more; "I don't care where you go. If you want, you could go to hell."

With that Henry stormed out of the room.

Mary, "come back here, Henry."

Henry screamed back, "hell with that girl. She is gone mad."

Mary, "I guess you are going to America, and we can't change your mind."

Katie, "it is already made up. But I have a question for you, Mother. Do you know how hard it is when your child does not speak to you for months?"

Mary, "no! But I know how hard it is when my own daughter does not want to bring my only grandson to stay with me."

Katie, "just multiply that feeling by a million. Mother, it is the worst feeling in the world. Until the subject of America came up, do you know that Josh only talked to me for maybe a full hour only one time? That was when he told me he wanted to leave everything behind. Remember, Mother, multiply that feeling by a million and you will know how I feel."

Mary came up to her daughter and gave her a big bear hug; "okay, honey. When are you going back to Ashington?"

Katie, "tomorrow. I was hoping that you would let me stay here for a night."

Mary continued hugging her only daughter; "of course, baby. You know I love you, and you could stay here as long as you like."

Katie had tears in her eyes; "I know you love me, Mother. Is Father going to be okay?"

Mary, "that old fool will be fine. But remember, he loves you, too."

Katie, "thank you, Mother."

Mary had one more question, "so, who is the father?"

Katie, totally dumbfounded, "Mother, what do you mean?"

Mary, "you know what I mean. You think I don't know. I have known all along. I am your mother, and I love you no matter what. You don't have to tell me who he is. But I have known all this time. I just wanted you to know that I once was young, too. I know how it feels to be young."

Katie, in shock, "Mother, I am sorry, but I can't tell you who he is. But when I am ready, you will be the second one to know."

Mary smiled and asked, "so who is going to be first?"

Katie, "Mother, I love you."

Mary, "I love you, too."

Katie, "thank you."

Mary, "I want you to tell me if Josh still looks the same."

Katie, "of course, he does. Still blonde as can be."

Mary, "so he still looks just like Robbie Kiel."

Katie just smiled; "well, Mother, you are amazing. I am going to go to my room."

As she went upstairs to her room, Katie had many questions on her mind. How did her mother know? How long had she known for? Has she told her father? Whom did she talk to? Did Robbie Kiel ever come by and ask for her? Katie knew one day she would ask all these questions to her mother. She knew one day she would get an answer. Katie actually felt relieved that someone else knew her secret.

Katie was done with the hardest part of her trip. She was relieved that she had told her parents her plans. She had been dreading this day for a long time. It was now over. She was ecstatic that she had gotten all of the stuff off of her chest. Her parents did not want her to leave and go to America just like she had predicted. But they knew they could not stop their daughter. After that discussion, Katie went to her childhood room and jumped in her bed. She lay motionless, staring at her ceiling for four hours. She thought about many things. She reminisced about her childhood. Katie realized those were her glory days. It was such a long time ago to her, but in her memory it seemed like yesterday. She thought about her first kiss, her first boyfriend, and, of course, the first time she had done that dirty deed in her room. Katie thought about her past and realized how stupid she was back then. She thought about her sweet sixteen party. She thought about all those sleep-overs with her friends. She wondered if everybody felt this way when they strolled back down memory lane. Even though she had done some silly things in her past, Katie enjoyed the great memories those days had etched in her mind. Katie knew she was happy back then. She was always happy growing up in this house. Her mother and father loved her. Katie always knew that as long as she lived here in Bedlington with her family she would be safe. Katie smiled at the plain white ceiling and hoped her son's childhood would be as happy as his mother's had been. With that wish, she decided to go for a long walk.

As she started her walk that night, Katie realized that nothing had changed in Bedlington. Everything had stayed the same in this town. The people were the same, and the houses were the same. In twelve years, time had not played its dirty tricks on Bedlington at all. It was cold outside. It became colder the faster Katie walked. She walked through the town and then went into the woods. She did not know to where she was walking, but she kept walking anyway. After thirty minutes in the dark woods, she was there. She had walked to the little creek where she and Robbie had created Josh. She found the same tree where the magic had happened twelve years earlier. Katie leaned back against the big oak tree and sat down. She closed her eyes for a couple of minutes and thought about Robbie Kiel.

Then, suddenly, a voice broke the silence from the background; "you can't be here, little lady."

Katie, a little scared turned around, "okay, I will leave. But I thought this was public property."

The voice responded, "no, ma'am, I own this property."

Katie thought that the voice sounded familiar, "do I know you, sir?"

The faceless voice walked a little closer to Katie; "I don't think so, little miss."

Katie got up from the tree trunk and approached the stranger slowly. With each step, the stranger's face was becoming clearer. Katie still was not able to make out the face in the dark.

Katie looked at the stranger with the hat and said, "my name is Katie Roark, I apologize for trespassing on your property."

The voice responded silently at first, looking straight at her in the dark, then said "well, Mrs. Roark, your apology is accepted."

Katie started walking away, she swore that she knew this stranger. Katie had turned around and looked at him several times but could not make out that familiar face in the dark. She had seen him before.

Then the stranger spoke up, "Katie, how could you not remember an old friend?"

Katie turned around quickly, "I am sorry, but I can't make out your face in the dark."

The voice said kindly, "That is okay. I sometimes wish people don't recognize me at all. My name is Robbie Kiel. A long lost friend of yours from a distant past."

Suddenly, Katie's stomach had butterflies in it. The hair on the back of her neck stood up. She had goose bumps on her arms. She did not know what to say. She had been dreaming of this moment for years. What would she say to him? Katie had rehearsed for this conversation thousands of times. She wanted to jump in his arms and tell him how not a day had passed in the last twelve years when she did not think about him.

Katie slowly approached Robbie and said, "it has been a long time, friend. How are you?"

Robbie responded with a boyish grin; "I am doing fine, how are you?"

Katie could not believe how much that young boy had changed; "I am doing excellently. I have been reading about you in the papers. You have done what you said you would do. I am actually very proud of you, Robbie."

Robbie smiled again; "thanks, Katie."

Katie did not hesitate anymore, she felt as if she had known this stranger her entire life, "I have a son Robbie, his name is Josh. He absolutely adored you for years."

Robbie, "I would like to meet him someday."

Katie breathed a little heavier, "I would like that."

Robbie, "what are you doing out here this late?"

Katie, "oh, I went for one of my long walks. I was reminiscing about the good old days."

Robbie, "no, that is not what I meant. What are you doing in Bedlington? I thought you lived with your husband in Ashington."

Katie, "my husband passed away a couple of years ago. I am here to see my parents."

Robbie was still inquisitive as ever. He had not changed at all in Katie's eyes; "I am sorry to hear that. How did he die?"

Katie, "he passed away from a heart attack."

Robbie, "what was he doing?"

Katie, with a smile, "playing football with my son."

Robbie, "is your son at your mother's? If so, I would like to meet with him."

Katie, "he stayed with my in-laws back at home."

Robbie, "that's too bad."

There was a silent pause between the two old friends. They both looked at each other and smiled.

Katie, "I came to Bedlington to let my parents know that I was moving to America with my son."

Robbie, "why?"

Katie, "we needed a little change of scenery. Josh took his father's dead very hard."

Robbie, "I understand."

Katie, "what are you doing here? Don't you have some big match to play the hero in?"

Robbie smiled, "I came to see my parents, too."

Katie, "forgive me for being rude. How are they?"

Robbie, "they are still the same. Nothing has changed."

Katie, shaking her head in agreement, "nothing has changed with my parents, too. They are still the same."

Silence took over again in that dark night. Neither one spoke. They just watched the other one as if they were watching a movie.

Robbie, "if you like, I could give you some tickets and you could bring Josh to one of my games before you leave for America."

Katie, "that sounds nice. But I don't think we would have the time."

Robbie, "that is alright."

Katie felt bad for shooting Robbie's idea down; "look, Robbie, I have to go. Good luck with your sport. You have done wonderfully for yourself. You have done everything you said that you would do. Not many people could say that about their lives. I have never been as proud of anyone as I have been of you. I hope you will win the World Cup one day and go out as the next Bobby Charlton."

Robbie smiled, "thank you, Katie."

Katie got closer to Robbie and gave him a hug. They held onto each other for a brief second and then Katie said, "you don't have to thank me. I admire you, Robbie." She kissed him softly on the cheek and walked away.

Robbie just sat there in the cold night on that same tree trunk that he and Katie had made love on years earlier and watched that gorgeous lady leave his life once again. Then something snapped in his head. He got up and started screaming.

Robbie shouted as Katie started to become more distant as she walked; "Katie Roark, I always wondered what I would say to you when I saw you. I wondered for twelve years. I rehearsed it for years. And one day I wrote you a letter and left it at your mother's house. You never replied to me. You never said a word."

Katie did not turn around. However, she stopped walking for a second and stood still. She did not turn around as Robbie continued yelling his thoughts.

Robbie continued on yelling as she stood motionless; "Katie Roark, I wondered and wondered what I would say. But I can't say it. I don't know how. However, I will tell you this. I always loved you. I thought about you every second of the way. Stop walking away from me. Turn around and tell me you felt the same way about me all those years. I know you felt the same way. I know you thought about me. I love you, Katie. Do you hear me? All you have to do is tell me that you don't feel the same way about me, and I will let my feelings go."

Katie continued standing motionless and then started walking in the dark.

As she walked she could hear Kiel yelling harder and louder than the previously; "Katie, I am not afraid to tell you I love you. I love you even though that might sound stupid to you. Tell me something. Respond to me. Respond to your admirer. Don't walk away and make me think about this day for another twelve years."

Katie did not stop walking; she continued walking faster. She started running and crying in the woods. She so desperately wanted to turn around and jump into his arms. She wanted to tell him that she too had thought about him for years. She wanted to tell him she loved him then and still loved him now. Katie knew she loved him from the very first day that they met. She had little Josh to remind her of Robbie Kiel everyday for the rest of her life. But she could not turn around. She had a little man to raise back home. He was just getting better. How would Josh respond to her mother dating somebody? How would Josh respond if he knew Robbie Kiel was his father? She had a whole new life ahead of her. She ran faster now. Katie was more confused then ever. Kiel continued shouting like a madman in the woods.

Robbie, "tell me you don't love me. Tell me you never thought about me. Tell me those things, and I will leave you alone forever. Everything I have done, I have done it for you. I did it so you would see me on television and come find me. Tell me you don't love me, and I will stop loving you. Do you hear me? Tell me you don't love me so I could stop loving you."

Katie ran and ran some more. She never turned around.

CHAPTER 14

❀

Trip to America

They were at the airport on a hot summer morning in 1992. Their flight would leave London and stop in Atlanta for a layover. From Atlanta, they would fly to Portland, Oregon and start their new lives. The whole trip would take a little over twenty hours. On that day, Josh was running around the airport. He was going from store to store buying candy. Katie could not comprehend how much energy little Josh had. He had not slept at all the night before. But Katie understood that Josh was very anxious. He was ready to go to America. She only hoped that her son would get tired enough to sleep on the plane. Their flight number was announced and they boarded their plane. Neither one of them had ever been in a plane, so they both marveled at this giant structure.

Twenty hours later, Katie and Josh Roark were in America. Katie had gotten her wish, little Josh had slept almost the entire trip. After a three-hour layover in Atlanta, they had made it to Portland. They were both very tired. At the airport in Portland, Katie flagged down a cab and they were headed to their new apartment.

CHAPTER 15

❀

Casey Taylor

Once Katie found out her little boy wanted to live in America, she had been wheeling and dealing. She had gotten herself an immigration attorney in order to take care of all the proper paperwork to reside in America. Katie had come in contact with the Law Offices of Casey Taylor through the phone book. She had made a trip to London and explained to Mr. Taylor her circumstances. She was impressed with how poised this middle-aged gentlemen seemed at their first appointment. Casey Taylor was in his early forties with a full head of dark hair. He was slender but tall. Katie had found him very attractive during her appointment.

Attorney Taylor, "how may I help you today, Mrs. Roark?"

Katie, "I am trying to move to America with my eleven-year old son, Josh. I am trying to find out what my proper steps are."

Attorney Taylor, "why America?"

Katie, "my son wants to move to America."

Attorney Taylor, "what about your husband?"

Katie, "he passed away about a year ago."

Attorney Taylor was very compassionate, "I see what you are trying to do. You are trying to start from scratch. It must be really hard for you and, especially, for your son, Josh. I know how it feels to lose a father. My father passed away when I was sixteen."

Katie, beginning to really like Mr. Taylor, "I am sorry to hear that. Josh's father passed away from a heart attack. If you don't mind me asking, how did your father pass away?"

Mr. Taylor, "I don't mind you asking at all. My father committed suicide. He killed himself one night. I was the first one to hear the gunshot."

Katie felt really bad about asking the question; "I am sorry to hear that. But I am actually happy to meet you. This gives me some hope that there are those out there who have lost fathers and still managed to survive in this crazy world of ours."

Attorney Taylor obliged, "thank you, Katie. Don't worry, Josh is going to be fine."

Katie, "how much is this going to cost me?"

Attorney Taylor, "with all the paperwork and with me expediting the whole process, it will come to five thousand American dollars."

Katie, "that is reasonable. If you could take care of everything by the first week of June, I will pay you $7,500."

Attorney Taylor, "I will make sure everything is taken care of as soon as possible."

Katie, "you have my number. Give me a call if you need anything else from me."

Attorney Taylor, "will do."

Katie, "thank you, Mr. Taylor. Looking forward to hearing from you soon."

In the next seven months, Casey Taylor took care of all of the proper paperwork for Josh and Katie Roark. Casey Taylor applied for their permanent residency, work visas and student visas for both Josh and Katie Roark. He had shown enough money in his client's account to the American Government so it was simple for the Roarks to get their permanent residency. By May of 1992 he had all the proper paperwork ready for his clients to travel to America.

CHAPTER 16

❀

Portland

Katie and Josh moved into their new home in mid-July. Josh was ecstatic about their apartment. Wimbledon Square had tennis courts and indoor and outdoor swimming pools. For a kid almost twelve years old, this was life.

Josh, running around the apartment, "Mother, this is great! I never thought America would be this much fun. I love you, Mother. Thank you for bringing me to Portland."

Katie, just happy as can be, "you're welcome. I am happy that you are happy, my king. Let's go swimming."

Josh, "I am ready, Mother. Let's go please, let's go now."

Katie, "let me go put on my bathing suit."

Josh, "Mother, hurry up."

Katie was unbelievably happy. Her happy little king was finally back. It had been two years since John Roark's passing and this was the first time little Josh was actually happy. Katie could not believe how happy her little boy had become. His happiness only made her happier. She had forgotten about all her problems in her son's immense enjoyment. Katie knew that as long as Josh was happy, she would be happy. If he was sad, she would be sad. Katie dedicated her life to this little guy. Little Josh was her source of pride and joy.

Portland, Oregon was breathtakingly beautiful. The people of Oregon were exceptionally nice. The first week they were in Portland, Katie registered Josh at his new school. Josh would be attending Sellwood Middle School. Sellwood was less than two blocks from Wimbledon Square. After registering Josh for school, they went to eat lunch in downtown Portland.

Katie, "Josh, are you excited about your new school?"

Josh, still all smiles, "yes, Mother I am very excited. I can't wait until I start school. I want to have a whole bunch of friends. Do you think kids will like me?"

Katie, embracing her son's excitement, "of course, honey, everybody is going to like you. You are going to be the most popular kid in school."

Josh, "I can't wait until I start seventh grade."

Katie, "I know, honey. But you must remember to treat everyone like you want to be treated."

Josh, "I know, Mother. I know your rules of being a good person."

Katie, "if you can tell me all my rules about being nice to people, I will get you whatever you want today."

Josh looked at his water glass and then looked at his mother; "1. Always be nice to people. 2. Treat everyone the same. 3. Be respectful to my elders. 4. Always help those that cannot stand up for themselves."

Katie got up out of her chair and went straight to little Kiel; "I love you, my little king."

Little Kiel replied, "I love you, too, Mother."

Katie, "so what do you want? I told you I will get you anything."

Josh, "can I get more than one thing?"

Katie, "as long as it is less than $100."

Josh, "okay, Mother, let's go to a shopping center."

Katie, "okay, my little king, just finish your food."

Josh continued eating, "yes, Mother."

That day Katie and Josh went to the mall. Katie bought Josh a baseball bat, glove, a baseball and an American football. During the next month, Josh made a lot of friends from his apartment complex. He was with his friends' everyday playing baseball, football and running around like a crazy kid again. Things were like the good old days at the Roark household. Katie and Josh were both happier than ever.

Two weeks before school started, Katie decided to buy a car. She went to many car dealerships and picked up a bunch of car brochures. She got back home and put all of the different brochures on the table. When Josh came into the house, he saw all the car magazines.

Josh, excited, "Mother, are we really buying a car?"

Katie, "yes, son! I was curious about what kind of car my king was interested in. Since we are a team, we will decide together."

Josh, "Mother, let's get something super cool."

Katie, "okay, but remember, we both have to like it."

Josh, "okay, Mother."

Katie, "how about a van?"

Josh, "no! I want something cool."

Katie, "alright! How about a Buick?"

Josh, "no, Mother! How about a Porsche?"

Katie, "son, let's be realistic. Porsche's are too expensive."

Josh, "how about a convertible?"

Katie, "okay, I always wanted a convertible."

Josh, "how about a Ford Mustang?"

Katie, "okay. We'll buy a Ford Mustang convertible."

That was the way Katie and Josh Roark's life started in America. Katie had decided that every important decision she would make would be brought to her little king's attention. Democracy was in full effect. She had two votes, and Josh had one.

CHAPTER 17

❀

All American

It had been six years since they had moved to Portland. Josh was now seventeen years old and a senior in high school. Everybody in Portland knew the name Josh Roark. He had been selected as Oregon Athlete of the Year for three consecutive years. In the history of Oregon athletics, that was unprecedented. An accomplishment like this was unheard of. His freshman year, Josh decided to run for the cross-country team. By the time the cross-country season had finished he held the Oregon state record for the mile and the three mile run. During his sophomore and junior years, he repeated as the state cross-country champion. Besides running and staying in shape, Josh decided to play one more sport his second year of high school. He gave baseball a shot. He was an unbelievable athlete. Just like in cross-country, he excelled in baseball. His first year playing high school baseball he had an E.R.A (earned run average) of 0.71 in the twelve games he had pitched. His pitching record was an unbelievable twelve wins and zero defeats. Josh not only pitched his way to a state championship, but helped his team with his amazing bat. He batted 0.765 with fifteen home runs. Like in cross-country, Josh had become an All State performer in baseball. Colleges started taking notice of Roark at the end of his sophomore year. Duke, UCLA, Stanford, Harvard, the University of Miami and the University of Texas were big name schools interested in him for their baseball teams. Tennessee, Michigan, and, of course, every other school in the country also vied to sign this magnificent prospect to play for their schools. Everywhere Josh Roark went people even wanted his autograph. His senior year came very quickly. By his senior year, Josh Roark had fully grown. He was six feet two inches tall and weighed 185 pounds. Not only was Roark an exceptional athlete, but just as good a student. He was number two in his class, and he had officially qualified academically to play any sport his heart desired in college. He scored a thirty-one on his A.C.T. This blonde Englishman had become a legend at Cleveland High School and in the state of Oregon.

CHAPTER 18

⚜

Teacher

Throughout her son's amazing run in high school, Katie also kept herself busy. In 1993 she enrolled at the University of Portland. At first, school was hard for Katie. She took the minimum course load to be considered full time her first year. Once she started getting used to schoolwork she increased her hours. By the time 1997 rolled around she had received her four-year degree in elementary education and started teaching at Grout Elementary School. She loved her new life. Her son was the state legend, and she now had a career.

CHAPTER 19

❀

A Legend Retires

Robbie Kiel played in three World Cups in his illustrious career. Yet he never won the thing he coveted most. The World Cup title had always eluded him. He was the European Player of the Year six times. He had led the Premiership in goals for ten straight years. Every individual honor he ever wanted he got. As the captain of Manchester United, Kiel won the notorious Champions League Trophy twice. Kiel had led United to eight consecutive league championships as well. In England and around the world, people could not speak of English football without speaking of Robbie Kiel.

In 1997, after playing his final game at Old Trafford, he stayed on the field and got on the public announcement microphone. Before the game, he had told no one about his plans. As Manchester United fans spotted Kiel with the microphone in the middle of the field, the whole place fell silent. You could hear a pin drop.

The blonde legend finally spoke; "I have been a member of this franchise for fifteen years."

The crowd acknowledged him and started clapping, whistling and chanting Kiel's name.

Kiel performed his infamous head gesture acknowledging his appreciation for the Manchester United fans.

The legend continued his speech; "we had our ups and downs: victories, defeats, heartache, and, of course, championships."

Kiel again stopped talking as the crowd reached a frenzy of chanting his name. Kiel again smiled his customary smile and acknowledged his fans.

> He continued speaking once Old Trafford went silent again; "I always knew I wanted to play for Manchester United as long as I can remember. I always dreamed as a young boy that one day I would wear the red United jersey and go out there and lead my team to many championships. I will tell you, all those dreams that I ever had have come true. I am a very lucky person for all of that."

Old Trafford erupted for the third time. "Kiel, Kiel, Kiel, Kiel, Kiel!" chanted the fans. Robbie smiled and waited for Old Trafford to quiet down once again.

> Kiel, "I have done it all. My only regret in my life is not leading my country to a World Cup Championship. The Manchester United fans are the best fans in the world, and I love you. I love Manchester United, and I love England. Today I am announcing my retirement from the great game of football."

Old Trafford went dead silent. Fans knew Kiel could still play the game at its highest level, and they were shocked by the news. They stood in complete silence and let the legend speak.

> With tears coming from Kiel's eyes, he continued; "it is time for me to retire. I am not as young as I once was. I am not as fast as I used to be. I just want you to know that I love Manchester United, I love England and I love all of you for loving me for the past sixteen years. I love you."

With the admission of his love, Kiel started walking from the middle of the field to the sideline. As he walked away from the game that he loved, his teammates ran up to their captain, gave him a hug and embraced him. Kiel started crying as Old Trafford chanted his name for the next forty-five minutes. As his teammates hugged him, the back-up goalkeeper and some of his other teammates lifted the crying Kiel on their shoulders. As he left the field on his teammates shoulders he sobbed like a little boy. He waved to the fans, and pandemonium broke loose. Robbie Kiel, the official King of England, left Old Trafford that night as the King of English football as well. Fans stayed at Old Trafford for the next hour and chanted his name. There wasn't a dry eye at Old Trafford that night.

In the Manchester United locker room, Kiel ran into his old friend, William Thacker. Of course, Thacker and his media buddies had filled the locker room waiting for a comment from the messiah.

Mr. Thacker, "why, Robbie?"

Kiel replied as he heard the echoes of his name being chanted; "I am getting old, Mr. Thacker. I am not who I once was. I am too old. There are so many young kids on this team who are ready to be superstars. Lately, I have been feeling as if I am holding them back."

Thacker, "but, Robbie, you are not holding anyone back. You led the team in goals again this year. You led the league in goals. You are still brilliant."

Kiel smiled, "thank you, Mr. Thacker. You have always treated me nicely."

Mr. Thacker, emotional, "I am telling you as a friend, Robbie. You are the best. Don't retire! You are still young."

Kiel smiled again; "I am young in life but a dinosaur in football. I love playing, but I know it is my time."

Mr. Thacker knew Kiel had made up his mind; "Robbie, I have only enjoyed watching one other player as much as I loved watching you. And you know it was your hero and mine, Bobby Charlton."

Kiel put his hand forward to shake Mr. Thacker's hand; "thank you, Mr. Thacker. You know you have always been my favorite. I want you to know that you are awesome. Thank you for all you have done for my career and English football."

Mr. Thacker got a little more emotional and reached over and gave the legend a hug; "thank you, Robbie, it means so much to me."

With that, Robbie Kiel hung up his cleats and took off his jersey one last time. He sat there for almost two hours until everybody cleared out of the United locker room. He knew this was the last time he would change his uniform as a professional player. Kiel picked up his jersey and put his face into his red number nine. Kiel cried and cried some more. The next morning, English newspaper headlines read, "English Legend Retires!"

CHAPTER 20

❀

Prophecy

Josh Roark had found out on the Internet that his boyhood idol had retired from English football. He tried to collect his thoughts and just stared at the computer screen. He was stunned. He remembered his father and the conversations he had with him about playing with Robbie Kiel. Josh sat there on his chair and smiled. He closed his eyes and thought about his childhood. How happy had he been then? How much had he loved his father? He did not think about his father as much in the past five years or so. All of a sudden, reading about his former hero brought back memories once again fresh. He promised his father he would lead England to a World Cup. He had promised his father he would be the next Bobby Charlton and then the next Robbie Kiel. He just sat there and thought about all of the football games he had gone to with his father. Reminiscing about his father made him sad. No matter how hard his mother tried to be both the father and the mother, it did not work. Nothing could fill the void inside of him. When he ran, when he played baseball, the emptiness of not having a father was always there. While his teammates' fathers would be at their sons every game or meet, his was only a memory.

Sitting there amongst his many trophies and accomplishments, Josh Roark decided it was time to fulfill the prophecy. He was going to play football again. He was going to try out for the high school soccer team and lead them to a state championship. Josh knew he would make the team. He decided it was time to lead England back to the most coveted title in the world. He got up from his seat, closed his eyes, raised his arms in the air and just imagined playing for Manchester United in Old Trafford. He imagined the roars. He imagined the crowd going crazy. He imagined leading the United to a Champions League Championship. Then he imagined leading England to a World Cup title. He imagined thanking his father as he held the trophy high. Then he imagined meeting his father's hero, Bobby Charlton. He wanted to tell Charlton how much his father had loved him. He wanted to tell Charlton that he was the reason he played the great game of football. As he imagined and dreamed, he saw himself meeting the blonde legend. He saw himself talking to Robbie Kiel. He wanted to tell Kiel that he was the greatest footballer he had ever seen. Josh opened his eyes and decided it was his time to leave his mark in English football. He left his room and found his mother in the kitchen. She was cooking dinner.

Josh, "Mother, I am ready to fulfill my destiny."

Katie did not know what her son was talking about; "what are you taking about, Josh?"

Josh, excited as ever, "what do you think about me trying out for the high school soccer team?"

Katie did not like the idea at all; "Josh, don't you think it will be too much? You are already on the cross-country and baseball teams. A third sport will get you too tired. You also have student council, homecoming and prom to think about. You are going to be overwhelmed. Have you decided where you are going to go to college? It is your senior year; you are supposed to enjoy it. I don't think you should play soccer. Too many things will be happening too fast."

Josh listened to his mother's reasons; "Mother, I know I have all those things to do. But I have to do this. I am going to try out for and make the soccer team. After that, I am going to play soccer at U.C.L.A (the University of California Los Angeles) for four years. I will make the first team All-America. After that, I am going back to England to play for Manchester United. My goal is to lead England to a World Cup."

Katie, still trying to change the boy's mind, "what about baseball? What about the Major League Draft? All the experts assured you to going number one in the draft. That is a million dollars in signing bonuses alone. Are you just going to pass it all up?"

Josh smiled; "Mother, don't worry! I am done with baseball. I have five goals in my life, and they all deal with soccer."

Katie, curious, "what are they?"

Josh, "the first one is to be an All-American at U.C.L.A.. The second goal is to play for Manchester United. Third is to play for England. The fourth is to win the World Cup in 2006. And the last one is to meet two people."

Katie, more interested as her son spoke, "so who are these two people?"

Josh, "Robbie Kiel and Bobby Charlton."

Katie just took a deep breath when she heard Robbie Kiel's name. She knew her son was stubborn and had already made up his mind. No matter how hard she tried to change his mind she knew it would not work. She knew for years this day would eventually come. And on this day, Josh's football fever would return. She knew that no matter what sport he played, football would always be his sport. Katie also knew that all the goals her son had just listed would come true. She had only met one other person that like Josh Roark: stubborn, persistent and goal-oriented. He was the boy's father. Katie started worrying, when he makes it to the biggest stage in the world, would people see the uncanny resemblance? Would they know that Josh Roark is Robbie Kiel's son? Surely so! Josh looked more and more like Robbie everyday. They were both six feet two inches tall. Both blonde with small noses and strong square jaws. They even spoke the same. Besides looks, they were both unbelievably modest. They had a certain kindness about themselves that only so many people possessed. Katie knew people would find out. She had to let Robbie Kiel know about his son before anyone else did. But how was she supposed to tell Robbie? Did she need to wait a couple more years?

Katie thought about these two questions and pondered. She would wait until Josh's senior year in college to let Robbie Kiel know about his son. This way she would see how good Josh really is. She was scared. However, she knew that with time, all wounds would heal. She would wait at least four more years and then figure out what to say.

CHAPTER 21

❀

Goalkeeper

His senior year, Josh went out for the soccer team and, naturally, made it. His soccer season went by quickly. With Josh leading the team in goals, Cleveland High School won their first fourteen games. Soccer scouts from all over the United States were coming to watch him play. This kid was amazing. Josh averaged three goals a game. The sheer number of goals he scored was unprecedented. During his fifteenth game, the coach of the Cleveland High School soccer team pulled him aside.

Coach Miller, "Josh, how come you didn't play soccer the past three years for me?"

Josh replied, "I wasn't ready."

Coach Miller shook his head in amazement; "you weren't ready. You are the best soccer player this state has ever seen. No one has ever seen this kind of size, speed, strength and stamina. I always knew you were a great athlete, but this is just too much."

Josh just smiled; "thank you, Coach. It means a lot to hear good things from you."

Coach Miller patted his modest superstar on the back; "you know, boy, if you only played the last three years, we would have won three state titles. You know, I never won a state title. My teams have always finished as the runner-up. But you are that missing link."

Josh, embarrassed by the compliments, "Coach, I will get you your state title."

Coach Miller knew he was in the presence of greatness. He could not comprehend what he was seeing, but he knew Josh Roark was special. The Cleveland High School soccer team lost one game in the next ten they played. Josh Roark had scored seventy-three goals in twenty-four games. The major Oregon newspaper, "The Oregonian," deemed Josh the greatest high school athlete Oregon had ever seen. Cleveland High School's regular season finished with twenty-three wins and one lost. They were the district champions and odds on favorite to win the state title.

Their first round opponent would be the Abraham Lincoln High School. Abraham Lincoln High School was the defending state champion. As the game started, they had two players shadowing Josh. It was a valiant effort on their part, but it was not enough. Josh was so gifted in soccer that he was able to easily pick apart Abraham Lincoln's defense with his pinpoint passing. Since two people covered Josh, he found the open man every time he touched the ball. Like normal, he still scored two goals. There was nobody in the state as fast as Josh. Cleveland High won five to two.

Cleveland High School advanced to the second round against James Madison High School. It was same thing all over again. The James Madison coaches strategized to try and cover him with two guys, but it was not enough. Josh still had his way. He scored three goals in Cleveland High School's three to zero victory. No team had an answer to young Roark.

Cleveland High's quarterfinal opponent was John Hopkins High School. John Hopkins had lost only two games all year. They were talented. A day before the quarterfinal game, Cleveland High School's goalkeeper had hurt himself in a freak accident during practice. This bothered Josh a lot. Jimmy Johnson, the goalkeeper, was Josh's best friend. Jimmy had also been Josh's next door neighbor for the past five years. Jimmy, also a senior on the Cleveland High School squad, was a natural athlete. As he came out of the goal on a one-on-one against Josh, they collided with each other. Jimmy was on the receiving end of the horrendous collision. His right foot hit Josh's leg and immediately broke. It was as if a firecracker had snapped. Everyone of his teammates heard the crack. Jimmy lay on the ground holding his ankle that just dangled from his leg. His pain was immense. Coach Miller and the team rushed Jimmy to the hospital. The whole team paced in the waiting area for four hours. Jimmy's parents were informed about the accident, and they soon arrived at the hospital to wait with the team. Josh's mother had also heard the news and rushed to the hospital.

> Doctor Smith, "Jimmy's ankle was broken. We had to operate on it. He is going to be fine, but he will be on crutches for six months with a cast."

> Josh did not hesitate to ask; "will he be able to play soccer again?"

> Doctor Smith, "of course he will. His ankle will be stronger than ever after the rehabilitation."

Josh breathed a sigh of relief. He had hurt his best friend and his future college roommate. They had many plans together. He blamed himself for the accident. Everybody left the hospital, including Josh's mother. But Josh stayed. He went into Jimmy's room and sat next to his buddy's bed.

> Josh, "I am sorry about what happened at practice. You know it was unintentional. I would never hurt my best friend on purpose."

> Jimmy, a little drugged up on morphine, "don't worry it, buddy; it happens. I don't blame you at all."

> Josh felt relieved; "thanks, man. I thought you would be mad at me."

> Jimmy, "why would you think that?"

> Josh, "I ended your senior season."

> Jimmy, "my leg would have broken anyway. It was meant to give out. I am lucky it happened against the best player in the state rather than some chump."

> Josh started laughing; "I guess so! You do have a valid point. If your leg had broken against John Hopkins, there is no way I could have continued playing."

> Jimmy, "see, buddy, you actually did our team a favor."

Josh was not surprised about how cool his friend was acting. Jimmy Johnson was the classiest person he had ever known. Jimmy did not use profanity and treated everyone with respect. He was like no one else. Everyone loved him. They had been friends for five years now, and Jimmy always was positive about everything. Even when his leg broke, he did not react negatively. He embraced the accident and moved forward immediately.

Josh, "thank you, Jimmy. You made me feel much better. Is there anything I can do for you before I go?"

Jimmy thought for a second; "actually, yes."

Josh, "what is it, buddy? What can I do or get for you?"

Jimmy hesitated for a second; "you can tell me something?"

Josh, "anything you want."

Jimmy, "I have been wondering since the beginning of the season."

Josh, "what is it? Tell me."

Jimmy, "here it is. Everybody in Oregon knows you as Mr. Oregon. Mr. Athlete-of-the-Year, everybody's All-American. You are awesome in baseball, in cross-country and I have seen you play in pick-up basketball games. I have seen you dunk a basketball like no other."

Josh, "so what? You are good at everything you do. What is your point?"

Jimmy, "I am trying to get to it. You know they gave me some morphine for the pain."

Josh started laughing; "I am sorry, buddy."

Jimmy, "why did you wait until your senior year to play soccer?"

Josh, "I don't know."

Jimmy, "come on, buddy, tell me. All those years you came out to watch me play soccer and never once did you touch a soccer ball."

Josh just shook his head; "I know, buddy. I know."

Jimmy, "tell me why you ran away from soccer."

Josh hesitated for a minute; "you know, Jimmy, I never talked about this with anyone but my mother. I tell you, it is hard to talk about."

Jimmy smiled, "we are best friends, and you just broke your best friend's leg. You have to tell me."

Josh started laughing; "alright then. When I was kid, my father had given me the title to be the next Bobby Charlton. I loved playing the game. I loved it so much that I ate, slept and dreamt soccer. My hero became Robbie Kiel."

Jimmy, "I know Robbie Kiel. He is awesome. You kind of look like him when you are playing."

Josh was very proud to hear that compliment; "thanks, Jimmy, that is the best compliment I have ever received."

Jimmy, "you are welcome. So what happened?"

Josh, "one day, on a cold, rainy November evening, I begged my father to go outside and play. He told me to go ask my mother. She said no. I begged, I became obnoxious and finally got my way. My mother got very upset with my father. They got into a big fight. But my father and I went to play. During the game I was up two to one. Father called me towards him and said no matter what happened, he would always love me. A couple of minutes later he fell face first and died right there in my arms. That is why I quit playing soccer. That is why I left England."

Jimmy, "it sounds like a movie. I am sorry to hear that. But you know it wasn't your fault."

Josh, "I didn't know for a long time. Then before this soccer season started, I saw on the web that Robbie Kiel retired. That day something happened. I don't know what, but, all of a sudden, I knew none of it was my fault. People just die."

Jimmy, "you are right, buddy. People just die."

Josh, "so that was the day I decided that I would fulfill my destiny."

Jimmy, "what is your destiny, Josh?"

Josh stood up, "to lead England back to a World Cup Championship just like my father's hero, Bobby Charlton."

Jimmy, "thank you for telling me all this."

Josh smiled, "anything else I could do for you?"

Jimmy, "play my position and lead us to a championship."

Josh looked at Jimmy; "I don't know."

Jimmy, jokingly, "if you can win the state championship as a goalkeeper, you will accomplish all of your dreams."

Josh started laughing; "I don't know about all that."

Jimmy just laughed; "you know I am drugged up. Go home and get your rest."

Josh shook his friend's hand; "I'll call you after the game."

Jimmy, "Josh, thank you for staying this long."

Josh, "no problem. Get well soon, buddy."

That night as he tossed and turned in his bed, Josh thought about everything Jimmy had asked and said. He couldn't believe he had confessed his deepest secrets to another person. He thought about all the things that had happened in the past twenty-four hours. The next day, before the quarterfinal game against John Hopkins High School, Josh pulled his coach aside to talk.

Josh, "coach Miller, I need a favor."

Coach Miller, "anything for you, buddy. Just name it."

Josh, "okay, Coach, just hear me out. Don't get mad at what I am about to say."

Coach Miller nodded; "go on."

Josh, "I want to play goalie for the rest of the playoffs."

Coach Miller's jaw dropped; "what the hell are you saying? Let me get this straight. Forty-five minutes before our quarterfinal game against the best team in the state, my superstar comes over to me and tells me he wants to play goalkeeper?"

Josh, "that is right, Coach, don't get mad. I know what I am doing."

Coach Miller continued trying to change Josh's mind; "you are the best player in the country, and you want me to let you play goalkeeper. You must think I am insane. Do you know there are at least thirty-five division one coaches here watching your every move? Look over there to the stands; that is the head United States soccer coach."

Josh, "Coach, I am aware of that. But I am not scared. I don't care about what those coaches think. I care about what you think. All I want you to say now is that you trust me."

Coach Miller just stared at Josh; "you are the best athlete I have ever coached, but I can't do this."

Josh, "Coach, I promise you, we won't lose. You will look like a genius."

Coach Miller shook his head in displeasure; "I can't believe I am even considering this. I won't let you do this to your career or my team. Look at the sideline; those are the U.S.A. national team coaches. Everybody wants to see Josh Roark dominate the field."

Josh, realizing he couldn't change Coach Miller's mind; "Coach, I hate to say this, but I have to. Either I play goalkeeper, or I won't play at all."

Coach Miller realized how serious his young superstar was. He knew there would be nothing he could say or do to change Josh's mind. He also knew that without Josh Roark's presence on that field that day they would have no chance of winning against John Hopkins. Even Josh Roark as the goalkeeper was better than not having him there at all.

Coach Miller, "okay, Son, go warm up."

Josh ecstatic now, "thank you, Coach, I won't let you down."

Coach Miller, "I know you won't. Just remember to have fun."

Josh went to the sideline and started going through his red Adidas bag. He pulled out a bright yellow number nine goalkeeper jersey with padding on the elbows. "Roark" was on the back of his jersey. Then he put on his goalkeeper shorts with black padding. He went deeper into his bag and found his goalkeeper gloves. Josh was now ready for the battle. As he changed into his goalkeeper attire, the whole stadium buzzed. Scouts and coaches looked at each other like it was a big joke. The John Hopkins High School team coaches sat there and watched in disbelief as Roark warmed up in goal. Nobody could believe it. The best high school soccer player in the country was going to play goalkeeper in the state tournament quarterfinal game. Nobody believed what they were witnessing. Nobody scored on him. Two days later, in the semifinal game, Josh Roark again played goalkeeper. He dominated once again. The fans of Cleveland High School could not comprehend how talented this kid really was. Exactly a week after his best friend broke his ankle, Josh Roark led Cleveland to the state championship game. In this game Cleveland High School beat Moss Point High four to zero and captured the state championship. Cleveland High had won three straight shutouts with Josh Roark in goal. "The Oregonian" read, "Josh Roark Can Do it All."

Josh found Jimmy after the final whistle of the championship game blew; "Jimmy, always remember what you told me in that hospital room."

Jimmy, all smiles and hugging his best friend, "I will, Josh, I will."

Josh was overjoyed in the moment; "thank you for being my best friend, Jimmy."

Jimmy hugged back his best friend and whispered in Josh's ear, "go get your World Cup."

In the three games Josh Roark played goalkeeper for his Cleveland, none of their opponents scored a single goal. Josh Roark had found his niche. His six feet two inch frame was just too much for any high school opponent, or even college opponent, to handle. He seemed quicker as a goalkeeper than anywhere else on the field. He was a tiger. Josh Roark had finally found himself a position that could differentiate him from both Charlton and Kiel.

CHAPTER 22

❦

Confession of a Legend

In 1999, two years after he retired from the game of football, Robbie Kiel was at the palace. Robbie Kiel was on the 1999 New Year's Honors List. He would be knighted by the Queen of England and given the title "Sir". Robbie had brought his mother and father along with him for this overwhelming honor. In his wildest dreams he never thought about receiving something like this. He had met royalty before, but not the Queen. It scared him. That evening Robbie received his honor like a true gentleman. He was modest and benevolent at the same time.

That night Kiel and his family stayed at his London apartment. His father spoke to Robbie for hours on the balcony as his mother slept.

Mr. Kiel asked, "Son, so when are you going to settle down and give us a grandson?"

Robbie, "I know, Father, I have been thinking about that for the last year or so."

Mr. Kiel, "is it that you couldn't find the right woman?"

Robbie just shook his head; "no, that is not it. I found the right woman years ago. But she did not want me."

Mr. Kiel, laughing, "what woman in their right mind would reject the great Robbie Kiel?"

Robbie, "Father, I have been in love with the same woman since I was eighteen."

Mr. Kiel stopped laughing; "who are you talking about?"

Robbie stared at his fathers aging eyes; "you don't know her. But she rejected me. She walked away as I confessed my undying love."

Mr. Kiel, "well, Son, you are a 'Sir' now. You are royalty. You can get whoever you want."

Robbie, "if only it was her. I still love her, Father."

Mr. Kiel, "if you love her like you say you do, you have to go find her tell her again."

Robbie, laughing, "Father I confessed once, and she did not love me back. She just walked away."

Mr. Kiel, "she must have had her reasons for walking away."

Robbie, "I guess so."

Mr. Kiel, "did she tell you that she didn't love you?"

Robbie, "no."

Mr. Kiel, "did she tell you that she didn't want to be with you?"

Robbie, "no!"

Mr. Kiel, "did she tell you that she hated you?"

Robbie, "no!"

Mr. Kiel, "then how the hell do you know that she does not love you?"

Robbie, "I don't know, Father. I don't know. She just walked away."

Mr. Kiel, "she must have had her reasons. You have to find her. You have to do everything in your power to make contact with her. You have to tell her how you feel. Even if this means that you look like an ass, Son, with love you have to throw yourself out there into the world naked. You can't be scared. Go find your love. Go find her, and hold her in your arms. Tell her that she is the one. Tell her as you hold her that there is no one else, that she has always been the one."

Robbie, "Father, you are pumping me up. Thank you. I will do this."

Mr. Kiel, "Son, it is better to have loved and lost than not loved at all."

Robbie got up and hugged his father; "I love you, Father."

Mr. Kiel hugged back his newly knighted son; "I love you, too, Sir Robbie Kiel."

With that statement they both laughed as they hit their booze. They had to celebrate. They had to celebrate hard. They both knew that they would remember this day for the rest of their lives.

CHAPTER 23

❀

Big Man on Campus

Josh graduated high school with his best friend, Jimmy, and enrolled at UCLA like he had originally planned. Josh had a full ride scholarship. He did not take any athletic scholarships. Instead, he went to college with an academic scholarship. He wanted to be known, not only as a great athlete, but as a scholar. He wanted people to respect his mind. Meanwhile, Jimmy went to UCLA on a baseball scholarship. His leg healed, and he performed better than he used to. They were roommates in athletic dormitories. Josh played soccer, and Jimmy played baseball.

After three years at UCLA, Josh had become the same legend he had been in Oregon. Everybody on campus knew who he was. He had led the Bruins to back-to-back-to-back NCAA national championships. In three years Josh played seventy-nine games. All seventy-nine games he played, he played as the Bruins goalkeeper. With Josh in goal, UCLA's record was an amazing seventy wins, six ties and three defeats. He had only been scored on for a total of ten goals in those three years. He was selected as the first team All Pacific Ten Conference player. He was also selected as the first team All American for three straight years.

Jimmy, at the same time, was successful in baseball. He took the Bruins to three straight College World Series. Although none of the trips resulted in a win, he was one of the most popular baseball players on campus. He had been selected to the second All Pacific Ten team for three straight years. Josh and Jimmy were having a blast in college. Their grades were great, and everyone like them. They were the two kings of UCLA athletics.

CHAPTER 24

❁

Meeting Kiel

Josh had come home for the summer of 2000. He wanted to live at home all summer just to relax and spend time with his mother. Katie had been teaching at Grout Elementary and was happy with her profession. One day that summer, around four thirty in the afternoon, their doorbell rang. Josh got up from the couch where he was playing "FIFA 2000" on his X-Box to answer the door.

Josh opened the door; "can I help you?"

The stranger had his back turned to the door; "yes, you may. Are you Josh Roark?"

Josh knew who this stranger was familiar, but could not pinpoint his identity, "yes, sir, I am."

The stranger extended his right hand to shake Josh's; "my name is Robbie Kiel. I am the head football coach for Manchester United."

Josh was in disbelief; "no, you can't be Robbie Kiel."

The stranger with his English accent jokingly asked, "I am bigger on television, aren't I?"

Josh started laughing, realizing it was his hero at his doorstep; "come on in, Mr. Kiel. Come on in, please."

Robbie Kiel smiled; "thank you, Josh."

They both went into the living room and sat down. Josh was a nervous a wreck. All these years people had worshiped Roark like a hero in Oregon. Josh had met many famous people never before affected by their presence. But here he was, like a little kid, just staring at Robbie Kiel as he ran around the room, stunned.

Josh, "I am sorry, Mr. Kiel, I have never been star-struck. I have met many famous people, and they have never had any effect on me. This is actually my first time all nervous and jittery like this. I don't know what has gotten into me."

Kiel, smiling as this kid spoke, "don't worry, my little buddy, it happens to me even now. I had met many famous people. They had no effect on me, either. But, one day, I met the Queen of England. I felt so nervous, so scared. I can't explain the feeling. But I understand."

Josh listening to his hero with his mouth open; "but you are Robbie Kiel. You are the most famous footballer England has ever seen since Bobby Charlton."

Kiel, smiling, "I know, Josh. But you are the most famous person in Oregon. I guess we are even."

Josh, "can I get you something to drink?"

Kiel, "sure!"

Josh, "I have Gatorade, Powerade, and soda."

Kiel, "you know soda is bad for you. I might as well live on the edge a little bit. Give me a soda."

Josh went into the kitchen, grabbed a soda and came back. While in the kitchen, Josh felt an amazing closeness to this superstar he had only felt around his own father years earlier. He couldn't explain why. But he thought, maybe because I admired him all those years, maybe that is why I feel so close to him.

Meanwhile, in the living room, Kiel took off his jacket and looked at the pictures. There were all sorts of trophies and pictures of Josh with his mother. Kiel did not know why but he felt a little queasy inside. He had immediately taken a liking to this young lad. He thought for a second, maybe I like him so much because he reminds me of myself with the same hair, same size, and the same look. Then Kiel thought about it for a second, I bet if I ever have a son, this is what he would look like. After a moment, Josh came back to the living room with the soda.

Robbie Kiel, "all these trophies are impressive."

Josh, very modest, "no, sir, they were all team efforts. I just got the recognition."

Robbie responded; "you have definitely done something right to have this many awards."

Josh, still modest, "thank you, Mr. Kiel, that means a lot."

Robbie corrected Josh; "just call me Robbie."

Josh, "yes, sir! Mr. Kiel."

Robbie started liking Josh more by the second. This kid had exceptional manners and was also very modest. He liked that. Josh knew how to present himself properly, as if he were an English Lord.

Josh, curious now, "how is United going to be this year?"

Kiel smiled; "we are missing a couple of major pieces. If things come together we will make a run at the Champions League, and, hopefully, win it all."

Josh listened to every word from this man very carefully, as if he were listening to God; "Mr. Kiel, I know United is going to do well. I know you are going to lead them to the promised land."

Robbie, "I told you, buddy, call me Robbie. No need to be so formal."

Josh, with an embarrassed grin, "I'll try, Mr. Kiel. But it is hard."

Robbie, "okay, don't worry about it. Call me whatever you like."

Josh, "I am your biggest fan, sir. I have been a fan since I was kid. I wanted to be you."

Robbie, "from what I understand, you are better than me."

Josh was very embarrassed by that statement; "oh no, sir. I am nowhere near as good as you. I could never be. You are the best. I can't compare myself to you."

Robbie smiled at the boy's modesty; "sure you can. If you work hard, you can do anything you want."

The door to Josh's house opened. Katie walked in with a couple of grocery bags in her hands. She said hello to Josh without realizing that there was another person in the room. She went into the kitchen and unloaded the groceries.

Josh came into the kitchen realizing his mother had not yet seen their royal guest; "Mother, can you come into the living room? I have someone that I need you to meet."

Katie, "come here, boy, give me a hug."

Josh gave his mother a hug and said, "Mother, come into the living room."

Katie, "what is wrong with you, my little king?"

Josh, "nothing, Mother, just come into the living room."

Katie, smiling, "you are acting like a ten-year old."

Josh, "come on, Mother, forget about the groceries."

Katie, "alright."

Josh walked into the living room, and the visitor stood up. He extended his arm and introduced himself.

Robbie, "my name is Robbie Kiel. I am the head football coach for Manchester United."

Katie's face had a blank look. She was shocked. What was Robbie Kiel doing in her living room? Did Robbie tell Josh that he knew her from the past? Surely not! Robbie Kiel was too classy of a gentleman to do something like that.

Katie extended her hand; "I am sorry for not saying anything earlier. I am shocked. The great Robbie Kiel is in my living room. Very nice to meet you, Mr. Kiel."

Robbie smiled his customary smile and said, "nice to meet you, too."

Katie, "can I get you something to eat, drink, anything?"

Robbie replied, "no, thank you, my little buddy already brought me a soda."

Katie ran around the house trying to pick things up; "oh! I am sorry my house is such a mess. I didn't know we would have royalty visiting us today."

Robbie, "no problem, Mrs. Roark. I apologize for coming without notice."

Katie gathered her thoughts, "no problem! But one does wonder, what is the purpose of your visit?"

Robbie replied, "in Josh's senior year, a scout from Manchester United was in America."

Josh surprised, "really!"

Katie, "for what purpose?"

Robbie, "he was here traveling across the country with his wife. He was in the states for vacation purposes."

Katie, still puzzled, "I see. What has this got to do with us?"

Robbie leaned forward on the couch; "Mrs. Roark, the scout's name is Lucky Burns. Maybe you have heard of him."

Katie, "I have heard of him."

Josh interfered; "isn't that the same Lucky Burns that discovered you, Mr. Kiel?"

Robbie, "yes, sir, he is. He watched your goal-keeping performance against John Hopkins. Instead of continuing his trip to Los Angeles he stayed in Oregon for one more week and watched your shutouts in the state play-offs."

Josh, "no way!"

Katie, "there is no way that is possible."

Robbie smiled; "that is why Jack Burns got the nickname of Lucky. He is known to find talent in unlikely places. Manchester United respects his football eye. He has an eye like no other."

Katie, "I see. So let me get this straight. Then Manchester United has been following my boy's career for the past three years."

Robbie, "yes, ma'am. You are right. We have been following him. We know the United States Soccer Federation wants Josh to play for America. They are willing to give you and Josh U.S. citizenship. The Major League Soccer draft is next year and Josh will go number one."

Josh interrupted; "Mr. Kiel, I'll only play for two teams. One is Manchester United and the second is England."

Robbie smiled at the boy's enthusiasm; "yes, sir, that is why I am here."

Katie, "why is that?"

Robbie replied, "we are weak at United in our goalkeeper position. I am the guy in charge. I want to win. I want the best goalkeeper possible so we can win. I am here to sign Josh Roark to play goalkeeper for Manchester United for this upcoming season. He will have a chance to start right away. He is good enough, big enough and, of course, he is ready now."

Josh just leaned back on the couch with a huge smile on his face; "I am ready to go, Mr. Kiel. Where do I sign?"

Katie knew this day would come when Josh was a little kid, "son! Relax we have to discuss this matter."

Josh got up from the couch went to his mother and gave her the biggest bear hug; "Mother, this is what I want to do."

Katie smiled at her boy. Then Josh went up to Robbie Kiel and gave him a big bear hug, too. They both turned to Katie and just smiled. Katie could not believe how much these two looked like each other. They could have been twins. She knew Josh looked like Robbie all those years but she never knew they were this identical.

Robbie turned to Katie; "we all should have dinner this week."

Josh, without waiting for his mother's response, "sure, Mr. Kiel. That would be great!"

Katie, "that is fine, Mr. Kiel. Just let us know when and where."

Robbie extended his right hand and shook Josh's first. Then he extended his hand to Katie. She obliged and shook his hand.

CHAPTER 25

❈

Doubting Kiel

They were at a fancy restaurant in downtown Portland. Valentino's was the classiest restaurant in Portland. They all came in a limousine. Katie Roark looked as if she were a princess. Even in her forties she looked gorgeous. As they walked into Valentino's everybody in the restaurant knew who this famous person was. Little rich kids approached Josh Roark and asked for autographs. For a second, Robbie thought the requests for autographs were for him. He had been so used to people asking for his signature over the years. But in America, things were different. People did not care for their soccer stars like they cared for their basketball or baseball stars. It was a different continent with different cultural loves. Robbie Kiel understood this. Robbie was actually happy that people did not recognize him here. He was tired of having the spotlight on him. Josh got up from the table to sign more autographs and excused himself.

Josh, "I am sorry, Mr. Kiel, it will only take a second."

Robbie knew it would take longer than a second; "don't worry about it, buddy! Hometown legends have to sign for their admirers."

Josh smiled and got up; "excuse me, Mother, I will be by the lobby."

Katie, "don't worry, Son Take as long as you like."

Josh replied, "I will be right back. Mother, please order for me."

Katie and Robbie stared at their boy as he walked away. Then they turned to each other and did not say a word for a minute.

Then Robbie spoke; "Katie, you look lovely tonight."

Katie, "thank you, Robbie."

Robbie, "you are more than welcome."

Katie, "so, Robbie, I want to know. Why are you really here?"

Robbie startled; "what do you mean?"

Katie, "cut the crap, Robbie, after all those years you show up at my doorstep, what should I think?"

Robbie, still startled by Katie's directness, "I don't understand what you mean."

Katie, "come on, Robbie. I know you made up that story about Lucky Jack. There is no way he could have spotted Josh. Josh is good, but he is not that good."

Robbie, "Katie, with all respect, I think you are giving yourself too much credit. I did not fly over an ocean to see you. I came here to acquire about the best goalkeeper in America."

Katie, still insisting, "Robbie, please be honest with me."

Robbie, "Katie, I am being honest with you. Do you think I am that desperate to come chase you in America?"

Katie thought about the question for a second and composed herself "I am sorry, Robbie. You are right. I apologize for snapping at you like this."

Robbie shook his head; "no problem, Katie. If you like, Lucky Jack could join us in about twenty minutes."

Katie, surprised, "he is in Portland, too?"

Robbie, "of course, he is. He is dying to meet Josh."

After five minutes, Josh was back at the table. He looked at his mother and smiled with happiness.

Josh, "have we ordered yet?"

Katie, "not yet, my king. We were waiting for you."

Josh, "I am sorry, Mr. Kiel. I just can't say no to autograph seekers."

Robbie, "don't apologize to me. I know how things are. It comes with the territory."

Josh, "thank you, sir."

After five more minutes the waiter came by. Waiters at Valentino's had white dress shirts with bow ties, black pants and black shoes. Josh's waiter was a Mexican fellow name Eduardo. Eduardo had gone to high school with Josh and they were about the same age. Eduardo recited the specials, and they ordered.

Robbie, to both Katie and Josh, "of course, there are some things we have to discuss."

Katie, "what are they?"

Josh, "I already said I would play for free."

Katie, "my little king, you have to more patient."

Josh smiled, "forgive me, Mr. Kiel, I am just so excited."

Katie patted her son on the head; "don't worry, Son. I understand your excitement."

Robbie, "you don't have to apologize to me."

Katie, "go ahead, Mr. Kiel."

Robbie, "as you know, this is first week of June. Our season begins in August and goes all the way until May. Our training camp begins in July. I have to be back in England in three days. This means, Josh, you could either come with me to Manchester in three days or you could fly by yourself next week."

Katie, "things are moving too fast, Mr. Kiel. We have much to discuss."

Josh interrupted, "Mother, do you hear that?"

Katie, "no, Josh, what are you talking about?"

Josh turned to Robbie; "Mr. Kiel, do you hear that?"

Robbie looked at Katie, "no, Josh, I can't hear anything."

Katie, "what is it, Son?"

Josh looked at both his mother and his idol; "it is the Three Lions roaring again. They have been waiting for forty years to roar. They have been waiting for me."

Robbie looked at this wild boy and realized what he was talking about. He wasn't just coming to England to play for Manchester United. He was coming to England to make the Three Lions roar again. Even sitting in Valentino's, hearing Josh's statement about the lions gave Robbie an adrenaline rush. He hadn't had this sort of rush since before he had retired. He could not believe what he was thinking. But the only thing he was focusing on now was to make the Manchester United European Champion again. After that, he would focus on taking over for the English National team. Kiel would lead England, with Josh as the starting goalkeeper, to a World Cup. Kiel did not say anything for the next few minutes. He just sat at Valentino's and pictured the Three Lions roaring the way they did forty years earlier.

CHAPTER 26

❀

New Captain

Josh had been in England for three years now. Just like in Portland, everybody knew his name in England, too. In the past three years, Josh had become one of the best goalkeepers in the world. He had led Manchester United to two Champions League titles and three Premierships in his first three years. He had become as big as Robbie Kiel in three short years. The media loved Roark. Now the media had Robbie Kiel as their coach and had his look-alike in goal. Josh wore his number nine goalkeeper jersey and the fans ate it up. This brought a certain level of comfort to everybody in England. People still loved Kiel. They also loved Charlton. Roark was a combination of both of those men. Wearing number nine made English fans adore him even more. Seeing someone that resembled so much of Kiel drove people closer to the game.

For the 2002 World Cup in Korea/Japan, Roark was the back-up goalkeeper for England. The starter for England in 2002 was a veteran goalkeeper from Liverpool. His name was Scott Johnson. He had been in the Premiership for a long time and he had played for England as their starting goalkeeper in the past two cups. Once England was eliminated from the cup race, the poor goalkeeper play was one of the hot topics that continued for months. People in England were infuriated when the head coach started the older veteran over Roark. However, Roark was the perfect teammate to Scott Johnson throughout the World Cup.

After England was eliminated from the cup, one of the reporters asked, "Josh, could you have done a better job than Scott Johnson?"

Roark, angered by this question, "of course, not. Scott Johnson is one of the classiest human beings I have ever met. He has been my roommate throughout the World Cup and I think he has done an exceptional job."

Reporters wanted sound bites from Roark, "are you going to be ready for the next World Cup?"

Josh replied, "of course, I will be ready. However, this does not mean I will replace the great Scott Johnson."

For a twenty-two year old, Roark said all the right things. He did the right things, and the people of England loved him for it. His teammates respected him as if he were a veteran. Throughout the cup, Roark did everything in his power to support the veteran keeper, Johnson. He knew his time would come in four years. This was Scott's time, and he respected the fact.

After not winning the World Cup in 2002, once again England made a change at the helms. They named Robbie Kiel, king of English football, as the head football coach for England. He would have four years to qualify England for the World Cup in Germany. Expectations were high. The English people knew if anyone could meet these high demands it was Sir Robbie Kiel. Robbie Kiel was the consummate winner. He had won at every level. He had taken Manchester United back to the top very quickly. He was a player's coach and players would do anything for him. If Kiel told them to run through a wall, they would try. That was the trademark of a Robbie Kiel team. The never-say-no attitude had led Manchester United to a successful trip to the top of the world's soccer ranks.

Sir Robbie Kiel was back at the national stage. After hearing the news of his new assignment to lead England to the World Cup, Kiel was honored by this amazing opportunity. He gave the first interview to his old friend, Mr. Thacker.

Mr. Thacker, "Sir Robbie Kiel, how does it feel to be in charge of English football?"

Robbie Kiel smiled; "nice seeing you, too, Mr. Thacker. You know, even after three years I can't get used to people calling me Sir Robbie Kiel. I have been blessed my whole life. I think this is one of the greatest honors I can have as a career football man."

Mr. Thacker, "Sir Kiel, you do know there was a lot of controversy over the goalkeeper selection in the past World Cup. What are you going to do at this position?"

Robbie, "I knew this would be one of the first questions you would ask. But I am prepared for this question."

Mr. Thacker, "well, what are you going to do, sir?"

Robbie replied, "as you know, Scott Johnson retired from international competition. I want to make it clear that I have the utmost respect for Scott Johnson and all he has done for English football. He has elevated the position of goalkeeper globally in the past twelve years. I played with him, and I love him. There isn't any other person that I would rather have in goal. If Scott was still active internationally, I would give him a shot."

Mr. Thacker, "what are your plans for the young Josh Roark?"

Sir Robbie Kiel, "I think Josh Roark is the best goalkeeper in the sport today. I think he has proven himself in the Premiership and around the world. He is a phenomenal football player. I will name him the starting goalkeeper for England, as of today."

Mr. Thacker, "how long have you been planning this?"

Robbie replied, "not long at all. Once I found out Scott Johnson retired, I knew Josh would be the next goalkeeper taking over the reins."

Mr. Thacker, "I am surprised."

Robbie laughed; "why are you surprised, Mr. Thacker? Don't you know he is the best goalkeeper in the world?"

Mr. Thacker, still baffled, "of course, he is. I am just surprised to see how quickly you have made your decision."

Robbie laughed a little more; "do you want another headline, Mr. Thacker?"

Mr. Thacker remembered the last time Kiel asked him this question in Mexico. He had delivered on his promise back than. Kiel had given a headline that had made Thacker very famous and credible.

Mr. Thacker, "yes, sir, I do want a headline."

Robbie, "tell England, Josh Roark is their new captain."

Mr. Thacker's eyes beamed in excitement; "thank you, Sir Robbie Kiel."

The next morning, the English newspapers around the country read, "ROARK IS THE NEW CAPTAIN!"

CHAPTER 27

❀

<u>90 Minutes of Hell</u>

By 2004 Josh Roark had established himself as England Football's premier ambassador. Roark possessed different levels of leadership. He was modest, kind, trustworthy and a born leader. He did not have to speak loudly for his teammates to respond to him. He spoke softly and carried a giant stick. Ever since he had burst onto the Premiership he had been successful. He never experienced a slump. Roark was always ready to play and always willing to do anything to win games. Both older and younger fans realized Roark's commitment to excellence. Of course, his amazing willingness to win reminded fans of Robbie Kiel.

Robbie Kiel won with Manchester United. People wondered if their favorite son could win with England. Starting with his first practice with the England national team, Kiel made things very clear. During an easy shooting drill where the defense set walls to block the free kicks, things were not getting done efficiently.

> Coach Kiel called in his troops and let them have it; "what the hell is wrong with you people?! This is the easiest drill in the world! Kids have been doing this wall for centuries. And they do it properly. How long have you guys been playing this sport? How the hell are we going to win?! Roark, you guys are an embarrassment to this game."

Josh did not know what was going on, this was the first time in five years he had heard his coach shouting like a madman at practice. In the past, if Kiel wanted to get his message clear he would speak softly and make sure everyone got the point.

Josh replied skittishly, "yes, sir!"

Coach Kiel continued with his rage; "what the hell kind of captain are you?! A simple defensive drill, and you can't lead this team properly. I guess I should call Scott Johnson back into the camp. Maybe he will do it right."

Josh did not respond.

Coach Kiel, "I have won almost all of the championships a person can possibly win. There is only one championship I covet more than any other; I hope you bums already figured out what that is. If not, you guys should all be sent back to your respective clubs and replaced by someone else who is willing to do the dirty work. World Cup is it! This country has not won it since the days of my hero, Charlton. World Cup Germany is ours. We will win the cup. We will let the lions roar once again. But the only way that is going to happen is with attention and execution to every minor detail. Does everyone understand that concept?

The whole team nodded and said, "yes, sir!"

Kiel pulled everybody in closer; "what is our goal?"

The Three Lions responded, "to win the cup!"

Kiel was obviously getting pumped, "how do we do this?"

The Three Lions responded, "attention and execution!"

From that day on, the message to the team was crystal clear. The Three Lions' motto was to go hard 110% every practice and every game. The goal was to win the cup. Even in tune-ups, the Three Lions went full speed. Never holding back, never taking off any time. Every minute of the ninety minute games for the English national team was spent in the highest effort. During one of the practices, Kiel uttered those famous words that would become his trademark for the rest of his career, "90 minutes of hell."

CHAPTER 28

✦

England versus Austria

September 4, 2004, Vienna. The opponent was Austria. After all of the friendly games England had played, it was finally time for England to officially begin their quest for the World Cup Germany. This started with the preliminary stages of World Cup 2006. England would have to play ten games. The top two teams from each group would advance to World Cup Germany.

England's game against Austria in Vienna was dubbed by English newspapers as "Kiel's Quest For The Cup Begins." The game began very shakily for England. Right off the bat, England was making stupid mistakes. England's sweeper, Martin Taggart, was playing horribly. He missed passes; he missed head balls. This was his first time in the preliminaries, and it was evident by his play. His poor play was contagious to the rest of the defense. Adam Osley, the right back, for England started making mistakes, too. The virus spread to the left fullback position, John Thomas Landry. It also reared its ugly head with the stopper, Derrick Correal. Before England realized what was happening, Austria had taken advantage of England's poor defensive play by striking first in the twenty-fifth minute. Austria 1, England 0.

Vienna was excited. The crowd was going absolutely nuts. England continued playing poorly. In the forty-second minute, outside of the English eighteen-yard line, Martin Taggart fouled the Austrian forward, and hard. The referee did not hesitate and went into his pocket. Taggart had become the first yellow card recipient of England in the qualifiers. England set up a five man wall with the directions from their captain. Everybody was covering somebody.

The Austrian forward looked at the wall and blasted one past the outstretched arms of Josh Roark. Austria 2, England 0.

In the next three minutes, England tried to play keep away. England was happy to go into halftime only down by two. As soon as the whistle blew, the English National Team left the field quickly for the locker room. The visitor's locker room in Vienna had a strange feeling. No one spoke. Kiel pulled the troops closer to one another.

> Kiel, mockingly, "that was a brilliant half. I thought we were going to get eliminated from the cup in the last forty-five minutes."

Not a single word in the locker room. You could hear a pin drop as Kiel stopped talking. Than he started using his second copyrighted phrase.

> Kiel, quietly, "what the hell is wrong with you guys?! You should be having fun. You people are the best twenty-two players that have come out of England. You should be playing with pride. Instead, you guys are half ass-ing it. What the hell is wrong with you guys?!"

Again, every time Sir Robbie Kiel spoke and stopped speaking the locker room was silent. You would think somebody died in that room.

> Kiel continued, "Roark!"

> Roark, "yes, sir!"

> Kiel started yelling; "both of those goals are your fault. If it weren't for your dumb mistakes we would be winning now. If you don't want to play the second half, just let me know. I will put in someone else who could give more effort."

Josh's roommate and best friend, Martin Taggart, looked around, humiliated. He made eye contact with his defensive counterparts, Osley, Correal and Landry. They knew what was going on. The captain was taking all sorts of heat from the coach because of them. With each tongue lashing Roark received from Kiel, the worse the defense felt. They knew they were going to play better in the second half.

> Roark responded, "Coach, I am sorry for playing like crap. I am responsible for those two goals, and I will make it up to my team."

Kiel smiled and remembered the first time he had met this young guy. He knew then this guy was special, and he knew now.

Kiel asked, "what do you think we should do for the second half, Roark?"

Roark stood up, "Coach, we need to play with a sweeper. Osley has to play sweeper, and Taggart has to play stopper. We need to move Correal to the right. John Thomas is fine where he is."

Kiel brought the men in closer and said, "defense, did you hear the changes?"

Taggart, Osley, Landry and Correal all nodded their heads in acknowledgment of the changes.

Kiel spoke, "we will come back from this deficit in the next forty-five minutes."

The Three Lions responded in agreement. The second half was a different experience for the Lions. They played hard football. They played mistake-free football. England was paying attention to every single detail and executing like never before. In the sixtieth minute, England struck with a goal from Walter Harrison. Austria 2, England 1.

After scoring their first goal in the preliminaries, England started playing even harder. It was visible that England was the stronger and better trained team. The English defense was amazing. Taggart seemed more comfortable as stopper and Osley was a natural libero. He reminded the English fans of Germany's Lothar. In the seventy-third minute, England struck again. This time on a cross by Walter Harrison to Jeremy Cooper, it was as if Harrison had picked up the ball with his hands and placed it on Cooper's head. Austria 2, England 2. In the next seventeen minutes, England played even harder. They were more than willing to leave all their energy in the field. Possession after possession, England attacked. Austria was willing to play for a tie. They pulled everybody back and cleared the ball every chance they had. England's first game in the World Cup Preliminary would finish in a tie.

After the game, Kiel spoke, "man, that was a fine effort in the second half. I am proud of you. You people are meant to be part of this great destiny of ours. We will win the cup. But the only way to win it is by paying attention to detail."

Roark asked if he could say something; "guys, I am proud of you for your second half effort, but I don't want to tie anymore games. I want to win the World Cup."

CHAPTER 29

❀

Letter

In the past, Katie would come see her son for two weeks and go back home to Portland. She was used to her life as a teacher. She traveled to England as much she could. On this particular occasion, after seeing England play Austria, Katie decided to visit her aging parents. She went back home to Bedlington. Mary and Henry still looked the same, just a little older. Katie hugged them and told them she was there to stay.

Mary, "I missed you so much. It has been almost a year since you were here last."

Katie, "Mother, if I could, I would come more. Between teaching and going to Josh's games, it is hard to make time."

Henry, holding her daughter close, "I missed you, my little princess."

Katie smiled; "I missed you, too, Father."

Mary, "how long are you going to stay?"

Katie, "as long as you'll let me."

Mary, "what do you mean?"

Katie, "I took some time off from school."

Mary, "how much time?"

Katie, "I decided to retire."

Mary, "why?"

Katie, "it is hard to travel here and then go back to America. Every time I leave I get sad."

Mary, "well, I am glad you are here. You can stay here as long as you like."

Henry, "how is my grandson?"

Katie, "thanks, Mother. Father, Josh is doing fine. They tied their first game to qualify for the World Cup."

Henry, "yeah, we watched the game here. The whole town was here to watch their two heroes. If you think about it, it is pretty crazy. Having Bedlington's best players side-by-side against the world."

Katie took a deep breath; "yeah, it is pretty wild."

Mary smiled; "people think they are twins around here."

Katie, knowing exactly what Mary was talking about, "who?"

Henry, "Josh and Sir Robbie Kiel!"

Katie, "yeah, they look alike."

Henry, "I wanted to talk to you about something for years now. I am getting old, and I might die soon. I don't want to go into my grave not knowing this."

Katie knew what the question was again but acted dumbly; "Father, you are never going to die. You are going to live long enough to watch Josh's children play football."

Mary, "we are getting older, sweetheart. He is seventy-three, and I am seventy. We won't live forever."

Katie, "what do you want to know?"

Henry, "years ago, before he was famous, Robbie Kiel used to come by and ask when you were coming home. I never thought about it back than. But he came by several times. Then we did not see him again for a long time. He was signed by Manchester United, and you know the rest of the story."

Katie, "go on, Father."

Henry, "well, I always wanted to know why he came by."

Katie, "we were close friends when I was going through a rough patch with John."

Henry, "I know that. But I guess you left an amazing memory for him. Two or three years after he retired from football, after he was honored by the queen, he came by the house."

Katie, "really! What did he say?"

Mary intervened; "he asked about the letter he had given us to give to you before he left for Manchester."

Katie, "really! Whatever happened to that letter?"

Henry, "I have it in my room. For three years we didn't look at it. And then, one day, Robbie became Robbie Kiel. We had to open it and take a glimpse at it. I am sorry, sweetheart."

Katie, "it is okay, Father. Not a big deal."

Mary brought the letter; "well, my sweetheart, that boy was in love with you then, and he is in love with you, still."

Henry, "I agree! The letter was amazing. You were married to John and had a three-year old boy. By no means could we have given you that letter."

Katie, "I understand you had your reasons."

Katie looked at the letter and went to go sit in the living room. Henry and Mary followed Katie as if they were kids. Katie pulled the letter out of its envelope and started reading it. As she read the first paragraph she got emotional. This was a young boy in love with her a long time ago. As she read the rest of the letter she smiled in utter joy. Robbie Kiel had confessed his undying love with beautiful penmanship on a piece of paper. This was almost twenty-three years ago, but Katie knew people did not do things like this all the time. Katie knew Kiel was special.

Mary, "well, honey, what do you think?"

Katie smiled; "I am speechless. This is the best thing anyone has ever given to me. This is like something out of the movies."

Mary, holding Henry's hand, "I know, sweetheart. A long time ago your father wrote a letter like that to me."

Henry, "yes, ma'am. I sure did. I don't regret giving you that letter one bit."

Katie, "when Robbie came back years later, what did he say?"

Henry, "well, he asked me if you ever got his letter. Of course, I said no. He asked me where might he be able to find you."

Katie, "what did you say?"

Henry, "I told him you were in Portland, in America. I told him that I had read the letter and that he should go find you. He should tell you how he felt."

Katie, "what did he say?"

Mary, "he just changed the subject."

Katie, "to what?"

Henry, "he asked about Josh. He asked if he was a good football player."

Katie, "what did you say?"

Henry, "I told him about Josh. I told him that before his father died he had been a big Robbie Kiel fan."

Mary picked up from where Henry left off; "he told Sir Robbie Kiel how all Josh ever wanted to do was to play for Manchester United, about how Josh was a wonderful talent."

Katie, "what did he say than?"

Henry, "he promised he would look into Josh's career. He promised that if Josh had even very little talent he would give him a chance with the United."

Katie, thinking deeply, "So that is how he got Lucky Jack to look at Josh."

Henry, "of course. Don't you remember? Lucky Jack was the one that discovered Robbie Kiel."

Katie stayed with her family for a couple of months and then went to Chorzow, Poland with her mother and father.

CHAPTER 30

❀

England versus Poland

September 8, 2004, Chorzow Poland. After the first preliminary game against Austria, English newspapers had a field day. The British Press wanted to know how a talented team like England could falter against a weak Austrian team. This was the hot topic in England until the Poland game.

Poland versus England started off at an extremely fast pace. Poland was playing remarkable football. They dominated the air against England. However, England had learned, after their first game, that ninety minutes of effort was what it would take to win games. Robbie Kiel had brought a certain swagger to the England National Team that had been missing for years. In the past, the England National Team was known as a bunch of royal pompous jack asses. Other international teams knew England would not do the dirty work necessary to win games.

In the tenth minute, England scored first. Jason Laird, England's sensational center mid-fielder, took a beautiful long ball from his stopper, Martin Taggart, with his chest. He brought the ball down and found streaking Jeremy Cooper. Cooper made a quick move to his right and put the ball into the back of the net. England 1, Poland 0.

From the tenth minute on, England's level of play went up another notch. Not only were they playing hard and picking up all of the garbage, but they started winning all of the air battles. At midfield England had Jason Laird, Brian Brazil, Joel Johnson and Bobby Wade. In Robbie Kiel's scheme of things, these players complimented each other differently. Up front at the forward position England had Walter Harrison and Jeremy Cooper.

In the thirty-third minute, Poland found a way to get back in the game. Derrick Correal, England's right fullback, made a mistake on a head ball and let the ball sneak behind him. In that brief second, the Polish forward who had been chasing the ball was rewarded for his hustle. Roark came out of the goal, but it was too late. The Polish forward made England pay for Correal's mistake. England 1, Poland 1.

The next twelve minutes got rougher between the two countries. England became more physical, and Poland retaliated. These twelve minutes made it clear how strong England really was. Instead of putting their head down after being scored on, they played harder. At halftime in Chorzow, the score was knotted at one.

> Coach Kiel, clapping in the locker room, "fine half, gentlemen. Fine effort. With each game we are getting better. Remember men, attention and execution make a perfect combination. Now I have a question for my captain."

> Roark, in the corner of the locker room, kneeling down on one knee, "yes, sir."

> Coach Kiel, "Roark, I am tired of answering for your mistakes the next day at press conferences. You are supposed to be the best goalkeeper to come out of England, but you are playing like you are still at UCLA. I want you to start paying attention to details. Do you understand me?"

> Roark stood up; "yes, sir. It won't happen again."

> Coach Kiel, sarcastically, "it better not. You are at an amazing pace. If you keep getting scored on a goal a game, you should be able to break every international game record we have."

As England started getting back on the field, Correal who had made that stupid mistake, approached his captain.

> Correal, "why didn't you blame me?"

> Roark smiled; "it wasn't your fault. It was mine. I am the captain of England, and I am accountable for every goal scored on us."

Correal knew this man would never blame anybody. He would take the weight of England on his shoulders and try to win the World Cup at any expense. The second half of the game began slowly for Poland. The Polish fans were singing and waving their flags around trying to encourage their team to pick up their intensity. But it was to no avail. Poland became sluggish in the second half. It was as if they were happy with a tie. They only sent one attacker and played conservative football the rest of the way. Kiel, realizing this, sent Taggart to play midfield. England was attacking with seven or eight players at a time.

In the seventy-sixth, minute Walter Harrison scored from a Taggart corner kick. It was as if Harrison had a magnet on his feet and the ball had found his foot through all the players in the Polish box. Harrison found the ball and one touched it into the back of the net. England 2, Poland 1.

In the next ten minutes Poland tried to attack furiously. It was a little too late. Roark and the English defense stood their ground. That night in Chorzow England took home their first World Cup preliminary win.

> Coach Kiel, "men, I am proud of you. You played a wonderful game. You represented your country well. From this point on we will not lose another game. We will always win. Now you know what winning feels like. You should want this same feeling again and again."

The team started a frenzied, passionate clapping and cheering. They continued clapping harder.

> Kiel raised his hand in the air; "the game ball goes to our relentless leader Josh Roark."

The whole team started clapping again. They were happy. Their captain was true a leader. He would always take responsibility for his team. He would never leave a player behind. The England National team knew this, and they loved Roark for it. They would follow him anywhere.

CHAPTER 31

❀

Telling the Truth

Back in Bedlington, Katie spent her days hanging out with her mother and father. She had always felt close to them. But now she felt even closer as they both got older. She thought to herself, as she took her long walks, maybe I feel closer to them because I know what it feels like to be a parent. Maybe because I am older. She wanted to tell them her secret. She wanted to tell them so badly she couldn't hide it anymore. She did not care. They needed to know.

Katie, "Mother, Father, can I talk to you?"

Henry, "sure, sweetheart, what is wrong?"

Mary, alarmed, "what is wrong, baby? Are you sick?"

Katie, "no, Mother, I am not sick. Thank you for asking."

Henry, "what is wrong?"

Katie, "I think we all should sit down."

Henry and Mary found two chairs and sat down. Katie found herself a chair, too.

Katie, "do you remember a long time ago when I used to come home all beat up?"

Henry, "yeah, this was before your husband stopped being a drunk. I wanted to kill him every time I saw your face like that."

Mary, "we hated him for doing that to you. He was an abusive bastard until you had Josh."

Katie, "that is right. That is what I want to talk about."

Mary, alarmed again, "is something wrong with my grandson?"

Katie, "oh, no."

Mary, "then what is it?"

Katie, "well, after high school I got pregnant and had an abortion. I hated myself for a long time. I thought for years that John and I couldn't have kids because of that reason. I hated who I was. I even tried to kill myself one time but the chamber was empty. Look how stupid I am. I couldn't even kill myself. What a dummy!"

Mary, crying a little, "go on, sweetheart."

Katie, "so I let that bastard John Roark just beat on me for my past mistake. I didn't care if I lived or died. Sometimes, when he would hit me hard, I only wished he would hit me harder and take me out of my misery."

Henry reached across the table to hold his daughter's cold hand; "go on, my sweetheart."

Katie, sadder as she spoke, "but he did not have it in him to kill me. No matter how much he drank, he couldn't kill me. He loved me in a weird way. We couldn't have kids, and he blamed me. He brought my self-esteem down. I hated who I was. Instead of beating on me, he would make sarcastic comments about not being able to have kids. Those comments were stronger than any of his blows. I would have taken the beatings any day rather than those sarcastic remarks."

Mary, crying, "what happened, sweetheart? Why did you decide to live?"

Katie looked at both of her parents and then said something they would never forget; "I met Robbie Kiel. I fell in love. I thought he was the greatest person in the world. He made me feel good about myself. Even with my busted up face and swollen eyes he made me proud to be a woman again."

Henry, "Robbie Kiel! The same Robbie Kiel that came to my house asking for that letter."

Mary, "yeah, stupid. How many Robbie Kiels do you think she knows?"

Katie, "yeah, Father, that Robbie Kiel. The one that you know, Father. The coach of England, coach of Manchester United. And, of course, the father of Josh Roark, that Robbie Kiel."

Mary, "I knew it for all those years. Ever since he brought that letter for you. I knew but I couldn't say anything. I waited for you to say something."

Henry, "what?!"

Katie, "yes. Robbie Kiel is the father of my son. After John died he left a lot of money for Josh and I to live on. That is why I left England. Robbie Kiel was everywhere. He was on television, on the radio and in every newspaper this country had. I didn't want to see him anymore. I didn't want to be reminded of him anymore."

Mary, "that explains a lot. That is why you never brought Josh to stay with us. That is why you never came to Bedlington."

Katie, "that is right, Mother. That is why!"

Henry, "does Josh know?"

Katie, "of course not, Father!"

Mary, "does Robbie know?"

Katie, "of course not!"

Henry, "that is why they look identical. England calls them their two favorite sons."

Mary, "are you going to tell Josh that his real father is Robbie Kiel?"

Katie, "yes, Mother but I don't know how."

Henry, "are you going to tell Robbie that he has a son?"

Katie, "I will, Father. With time I will tell them both."

CHAPTER 32

❀

Love

On the trip back to England from Poland, Robbie Kiel wanted to see his captain on the team plane.

Josh, "Coach, you wanted to see me?"

Robbie Kiel, "Josh, how are you?"

Josh smiled: "I am fine. If we keep winning, I will be better."

Robbie Kiel smiled back; "I see. So winning makes you happy."

Josh smiled again; "of course, it does. All I care about now is winning the World Cup."

Robbie, "what are you going to do after we win?"

Josh, "I am going to retire from football and go back to America."

Robbie, a little puzzled by this, "but you love football. Why would you want to quit?"

Josh, "I love football. I love Manchester United. I love playing for England. But I am getting older. I have different interests."

Robbie realized he had never discussed his player's personal life; "what are your interests?"

Josh, "I want to go back and get my degree in physics. After that, I would like to go to medical school and become a doctor."

Robbie, impressed by his captain's future plans, "I see. Let me get this straight, you are just going to retire after we win, no strings attached?"

Josh, "yes, sir, I am. With no strings attached. Think about this, Coach, I have won at every level. The only thing keeping me around is winning the World Cup."

Robbie asked, "why do you want to win the World Cup so badly?"

Josh, "I made a promise to my father a long time ago. I told him I would play for Manchester United. I fulfilled that promise. I told him I would play for England, and, of course, I accomplished that."

Robbie, "I see. You have one more goal to accomplish."

Josh, "yes, sir. One more and I am done."

Robbie, "what is that final goal?"

Josh, "to win the World Cup. Then my life will be complete."

Robbie, "forgive me if I am being intrusive, but do you have a romantic interest? A girlfriend perhaps?"

Josh smiled; "coach you are not being intrusive at all. I am in love with someone back in America. She does not know my intentions, but I am in love with her. I think about her all the time."

Robbie, "what is her name?"

Josh, "Lisa Harper!"

Robbie, "pretty name. What does she look like?"

Josh, "she is a blonde gorgeous girl with a beautiful smile."

Robbie, "does she know you love her?"

Josh, "I never had the courage to tell her. We are not even friends. We were classmates back at UCLA."

Robbie, "how come you never asked her out for a date?"

Josh, "we have been acquaintances, and I was scared. I did not want her to say no to me."

Robbie, "I understand."

Josh, "do you want to hear a funny thing, Coach?"

Robbie smiled; "of course, I do."

Josh, "this one time I sent her flowers at the restaurant she worked. I did not even put my name on the card."

Robbie, "what did the card say?"

Josh, "she had just gotten a job with a big corporation. She had told me during the week that she was very excited. So the card said, "I hope you like the flowers. Good luck at your new job." How stupid!"

Robbie, "that is not stupid at all. You should have put your name on the card. But don't worry. Years from now, you will look back and laugh about it."

Josh, "maybe. But when I go back to Los Angeles I am going to find her and ask her out."

Robbie, "that is the Josh Roark I know. Fearless and persistent."

Josh smiled, "thanks, Coach."

Robbie, "I have a question for you."

Josh, "what is it?"

Robbie, "would you mind if I ask your mother out to dinner?"

Josh smiled and mockingly said, "Coach, do you have a crush on my mother?"

Robbie, "I think she is very classy."

Josh, "I don't mind at all. If she says yes then good luck. She hasn't been on a date in a long time."

Robbie, "this wouldn't affect our relationship, would it?"

Josh, "no, Coach, why would it?"

Robbie, "we are both public figures. The tabloids will have a field day with this one."

Josh, "I stopped worrying about what others said about me at age twelve."

Robbie, "you wouldn't have a problem with me asking her out then?"

Josh, "no! Not it at all."

Robbie, "will it be a distraction?"

Josh, "what do you mean?"

Robbie, "will it affect the way you play?"

Josh, "Coach, I am a professional. Nothing will affect the way I play. Once I step on the field I am in a happy place. I forget everything for ninety minutes."

Robbie, "alright then. I will ask her out."

Josh, "good luck! I hope things work out for the best."

Robbie patted his captain on the shoulder as he walked back to his seat; "thank you, Josh."

Josh smiled and said, "thanks for listening."

CHAPTER 33

❈

Phone Call

A week before England played Wales in Manchester, Robbie Kiel called Katie Roark at her parents' house.

Robbie, on the phone, "this is Robbie Kiel, may I speak to Katie Roark?"

Katie, on the other end, "this is Katie."

Robbie, "hey, Katie, how are you?"

Katie, "I am doing wonderfully. How about you?"

Robbie, "I am doing great."

Katie jokingly; "have you been keeping an eye on my boy?"

Robbie laughed; "of course, I am. He is our captain."

Katie, "are we going to beat Wales."

Robbie, "I certainly hope so. It is going to be a tough game. But we are at home in front of our great crowd. That is always a plus."

Katie, "are you going to send us some tickets?"

Robbie, "of course! How many do you need?"

Katie, "five! I am going to bring my mother, father and my in-laws."

Robbie, "that is no problem. I will give you and your family my box seats. You will be sitting with my mother and father. Is that okay?"

Katie smiled on the phone; "of course, it is. I have always wanted to meet them."

Robbie, "I will introduce you to them after the game."

Katie, "that is great."

Robbie, "Katie, I asked Josh if it would be okay to ask you out, and he said yes."

Katie smiled; "did he?"

Robbie, "yes, ma'am, he sure did."

Katie, "are you going to ask me out?"

Robbie, "yes, I am. Would you like to do dinner sometime next week? After all of the football hoopla dies down a little bit."

Katie, "I would love that."

Robbie, "okay, it is a date."

Katie, "it is a date. Sometime next week, call me, and let me know when."

Robbie, "okay. Tell your family I said hello. I will see you after the Wales game."

Katie, "okay, Robbie."

Robbie, "it was nice to talking to you."

Katie, "likewise."

CHAPTER 34

❀

England versus Wales

September 9, 2004, Manchester, England. This was England's first home game in the World Cup preliminaries. England's opponent in Old Trafford was Wales. Football pundits had picked Wales as one of the weaker teams in England's group. Everybody in England knew this would be an easy game.

For England, the game started very quickly. In the second minute, England got a corner kick. Jason Laird, England's top mid-fielder, took the kick. Laird's cross landed in front of Harrison. Harrison took a shot and the ball ricocheted off of the Wales goalkeeper. The ball rolled outside of the eighteen where it found the right leg of Brian Brazil. As soon as Brazil received the ball he took a hard shot. The ball sailed over the diving goalkeeper and landed in Wales net. England 1, Wales 0. Old Trafford was filled with enthusiasm. The English fans were louder than ever. Fans sang and waved their English scarves and towels. It was pandemonium.

In the twelfth minute, England missed a sure opportunity. Jason Laird and Brian Brazil worked together on a perfect wall pass. All of a sudden, as a result of this pass by Brazil, Laird was one-on-one with the goalkeeper. He chipped it over the oncoming goalkeeper who was trying to close his angle in order to save Laird's shot. Laird's chip sailed over the empty goal. For that brief instance, it seemed as if life had been sucked out of Old Trafford. In the next ten minutes, down by one goal, Wales attacked. They were relentless in their efforts. Roark was amazing in goal. He saved shot after shot. After gaining control of the ball, Roark pointed at his forwards, Walter Harrison and Jeremy Cooper, to keep going up farther. He also instructed his mid-fielders to move forward into the Wales eighteen. Roark released a monster punt. The ball sailed across the midfield and landed around the Wales eighteen-yard area. There, England took control of the ball and released another massive shot. This time it was Walter Harrison. Harrison's shot recoiled off one of the Wales' defenders and found the back of the net. England 2, Wales 0. Old Trafford was hungry for more. The stadium was loud as it could be.

The first half ended with that score. The second half was more of the same. England attacked and attacked some more. The best highlight of the second half belonged to Josh Roark. He saved a penalty kick. According to all of England's fans, it was an unintentional foul by Martin Taggart in the English box. However, the head linesman saw it in a different way. He gave a yellow card to Taggart and awarded the Wales National Team a penalty kick.

> Roark realized Taggart had his head down. He approached him and said, "good hustle, Martin. Don't worry about the foul. Just keep your head up. I will take care of the rest."

The Wales forward lined up and took a shot to Josh's right. Josh dove and punched the ball out towards the corner flag with cat-quick reflexes. Old Trafford chanted their hero's name for the next five minutes as the game continued. England had won their second game in a row. The whole country was proud of their national team. They had won two out of their first three contests. The only blemish on their record was the tie against Austria.

CHAPTER 35

✾

Lisa Harper

After the Wales game, Josh Roark was called into Robbie Kiel's office. Josh did not know what was going on. He was actually kind of nervous. In the past, it would be Kiel who would call him into his office, but now it was one of the assistant coaches that told Josh Kiel wanted to see him.

Roark knocked on the door. On the other side of the door he heard Kiel speak; "come in, please."

Josh, "Coach, you wanted to see me?"

Kiel, "yes, Josh, sit down."

Josh, "is there something wrong?"

Kiel, "no! I just wanted to let you know how proud I am of you as this country's captain."

Josh did not know what to say; "I am honored to receive such a compliment, let alone from my hero. Thank you, sir."

Kiel, "it is my pleasure."

Josh, "thank you, Coach. To have the honor to play for Sir Robbie Kiel is unbelievable. I have been truly blessed. You are the only coach I have ever had since I came to England. We have always been winners. It is because of you, sir."

Kiel, "I hope you don't mind, but I have done something out of the ordinary."

Josh smiled; "Coach, whatever you did, I am okay with it. I trust your judgement."

Kiel opened one of his drawers. He reached in and picked up a piece of paper. He leaned forward and gave Josh the paper.

Josh, "what is this?"

Kiel, "it is a phone number."

Josh, "for whom?"

Kiel, "for Lisa Harper!"

Josh, "my Lisa Harper?"

Kiel, "yes, sir."

Josh, "how did you find this?"

Kiel, "I have my researchers. I want you to call her after we get back from Azerbaiijan."

Josh, "that is crazy, Coach. I haven't spoken to this girl in years."

Kiel, "that is not crazy at all. What is crazy is you not calling her. That is crazy."

Josh, "Coach, it is a waste of time. What if she is married? What if she has a boyfriend? What if she is engaged?"

Kiel, "according to my sources, she is none of those things. She is as single as can be."

Josh, "okay, let's say I'll call her. But what do I say?"

Kiel, "tell her you were the one that sent her those flowers."

Josh smiled; "okay."

The next morning Josh Roark pondered whether or not he should call Lisa Harper. He thought about Robbie's advice and decided he should call her. But he had several questions on his mind. What if she didn't know who he was? What if she thought he was some sort of stalker? What if she thought he was insane? He could make a total jackass out of himself. Josh deliberated for a long time and figured the time difference between England and Los Angeles. He decided to call. He dialed her number as his heart pounded. He waited for about ten seconds.

A female voice answered; "hello?"

Josh, "this is Josh Roark. May I speak to Lisa?"

The female voice responded, "this is Lisa."

Josh did not know what to say, "hi, Lisa, I don't think you remember me, but I used have a physics class with you at UCLA."

Lisa, "I remember your name, it sounds familiar but I can't make out your face."

Josh, "sorry. It has been a long time. I should have called you years earlier."

Lisa, realizing Josh's uneasiness, "I remember now. You were the big soccer player here. Then, all of a sudden, you disappeared."

Josh, a little less anxious, "yeah, I left before my senior year."

Lisa, "what happened? Did you quit playing soccer?"

Josh, "no, I decided to follow my dreams and play on the next level."

Lisa, "what level is that?"

Josh, "I play for Manchester United and England."

Lisa, mockingly, "no way! I remember people talking about how good you were, but you can't be that good."

Josh, "well do you want me to prove it to you?"

Lisa, laughing, "sure! But how?"

Josh, "do you have Internet access?"

Lisa, "I do!"

Josh, "go to the Manchester United website, and look for the team picture."

Lisa, a little more serious now, "you aren't joking."

Josh, "of course not."

Lisa did her search on the Internet and found Manchester United. On that website she found the Manchester United team picture.

Lisa, "oh my gosh! You were serious!"

Josh laughed; "of course I am! Why would I lie?"

Lisa, "I am sorry. I thought you were joking for a second. I thought maybe this was a prank."

Josh smiled; "it is alright."

There was silence over the phone for about thirty seconds. To Josh and Lisa those thirty seconds felt like an eternity.

Lisa, "well, are you as good as this web site makes you out to be?"

Josh responded quickly; "no, that's not it at all. Don't believe the hype!"

Lisa smiled; "you are quiet modest for someone very well known."

Josh, "thank you. Enough about me, what do you do?"

Lisa, "I became an optometrist."

Josh, "that is impressive. I guess I should call you Dr. Harper."

Lisa laughed; "no need for titles."

Josh, "I am going to be in Los Angeles for the weekend. Would you like to go out and have some coffee with me?"

Lisa thought about it for a second and then said, "sure!"

Josh, "Saturday afternoon sound good to you?"

Lisa, "that sounds great."

Josh, "I'll see you Saturday. I'll call you when I am in Los Angeles."

Lisa, "okay, see you Saturday."

On Friday Josh went up to the team owner for Manchester United and asked if he could catch a ride to America with one of the team's Concorde's. He explained to the owner it was for personal reasons, and he would be back on Sunday. Without any hesitation, Josh's wish was granted. After all, Josh Roark was the most coveted star in England and, this was the first time he had ever asked for a favor.

CHAPTER 36

❀

Date with Lisa

On Saturday morning Josh called Lisa. He asked her for directions. Once he got the directions he told her that he would be at her place by noon. All morning, even after the conversation with the girl of his dreams, he was nervous. He could not wait until twelve. At noon Josh pulled up to Lisa's driveway. He got out of his rented Volvo and knocked on the door.

Lisa opened the door; "hello, Josh, come in please. It is going to take me a couple of minutes."

Josh, "thank you."

Lisa, "make yourself at home."

Josh, "thanks."

Lisa, "there is bottled water and soft drinks in the fridge."

Josh, "I am fine, thank you."

In less than five minutes Dr. Harper was ready to go. Josh walked outside and waited for Lisa as she locked her door. Lisa looked gorgeous. Josh waited for her to come towards the car and then opened the door for her.

Lisa, "thank you, Josh."

Josh, "you are welcome."

Josh went around the car and got into the driver's seat. He turned on the ignition and backed out of the driveway.

Josh, "Dr. Harper, where are we going?"

Lisa, "come on, Josh, no need for titles."

Josh smiled; "I am sorry, Lisa."

Lisa smiled back; "no problem."

Josh, "where would you like to do lunch?"

Lisa, "it doesn't matter to me. Wherever you like."

Josh, "I haven't been in Los Angeles in a long time, so I will let you make the decisions. I wouldn't know what is good and what is not."

Lisa, "do you like Chinese food?"

Josh, "sure!"

Lisa, "do you like Italian food?"

Josh, "sure!"

Lisa, "I know this great Italian restaurant in downtown."

Josh, "is the food any good?"

Lisa, "I heard it was marvelous."

Josh, "what is the name of the restaurant?"

Lisa smiled; "Italiannis!"

Josh and Lisa both shared a quick laugh. They ate at Italiannis. The whole afternoon they talked about anything and everything. It was as if they had known each other forever. Around nine o'clock that night they stopped for dinner at a fancy Beverly Hills restaurant called Mary's Place.

Lisa, "Josh, are you sure you want to eat here?"

Josh, "yeah, I am pretty sure."

Lisa, "this is where Hollywood stars eat."

Josh acted as if he did not know; "oh, really."

Lisa, "you would need reservations for this place at least a month ahead of time."

Josh smiled; "really?"

Lisa, "of course. This place is for royalty. I don't even think we are properly dressed."

Josh smiled; "don't worry; I have everything taken care of."

They walked into the restaurant, and the host immediately took the couple to their private seat without asking any questions.

Lisa, "what was that about?"

Josh, "what?"

Lisa, "he didn't even ask our name."

Josh smiled; "he probably confused us with someone else."

Lisa, "maybe! But I doubt it."

They both started looking at the menu. Lisa kept on flipping the pages of the menu while Josh looked at the wine list.

Lisa, "Josh, look I am doctor. I make very good money. This place is very expensive. This place doesn't even have any prices on any of their food."

Josh, ignoring Lisa, "do you like champagne?"

Lisa, "what?"

Josh, "do you like red wine, white wine or champagne?"

Lisa, "let's do champagne."

Josh, "no problem."

Josh turned to the waiter, who had been standing frozen behind him for the past five minutes and said to him, "bring me your best champagne."

A minute later the waiter brought out the champagne. He poured the champagne for both of them.

Josh, "I'll let the lady taste it first."

Lisa tasted the champagne, "oh my gosh, this is amazing."

Josh, "thanks."

They looked at the menu for ten more minutes, and then they ordered. Josh and Lisa sat there and talked while they waited for their food. During their stay at the table, someone had sent another bottle of champagne to them.

Josh asked the waiter, "who is this from?"

The waiter replied, "it is from the older gentleman two tables down from us, sir."

Josh made eye contact and nodded towards the gentleman. Ten minutes later the stranger in his tuxedo walked towards Josh's and Lisa's table.

Josh, "thank you for the champagne, sir."

The stranger replied, "think nothing of it, sir. I just wanted you to know I am your biggest fan. You are the pride of England."

Josh replied, "thank you, sir. I have been a big fan of yours for years. I love your movies."

The stranger reached out to Lisa with his right hand to shake hers; "take care of this young man; he is a king where I am from."

Lisa was mesmerized by the moment, but gathered her thoughts quickly; "I sure will."

The older gentleman released her hand; "it was nice to talking to you both."

Lisa smiled as if she were a kid again, "the pleasure is mine."

The famous actor apologized for bothering the superstar and walked back to his table. Lisa was still shocked by the moment.

Lisa to Josh, "he is a fan of yours. Do you know who he is?"

Josh, "I guess he is a fan of mine. This is the first time I met him. Did you see him in *Silence of the Lambs*?"

Lisa, "of course, I did. He is a great actor. I see all his movies. Are you pretty big in England?"

Josh smiled and said, "no!"

Lisa smiled back at this handsome man; "you are very modest for a famous person."

Josh smiled; "thank you, Lisa. If you don't mind me saying so, you are beautiful."

By midnight they were still at the restaurant. Josh asked for the check. It was a cue for the waiter. Several minutes later, the waiter arrived back with pink tulips.

Josh, "these are for you. I hope you like them."

Lisa, "oh my gosh, thank you so much! These are gorgeous. I love tulips!"

Josh, "read the card, please."

Lisa, "okay." Lisa started reading the card; "I hope you like the flowers. Congratulations on your new job."

She knew years earlier she had received flowers from an admirer with no name, but the card had read the same thing.

Lisa, "it was you who sent me those pink tulips years earlier."

Josh nodded; "yes, it was."

That night Josh took her home and dropped her off in front of her house. He gave her a hug.

Lisa, "I had a great time."

Josh, "me, too. I hope we can do it again sometime."

Lisa, "I sure hope so."

Josh, "I have to go back to England tomorrow. But I will call you very soon."

Lisa smiled; "I am looking forward to it."

Josh leaned forward and kissed her soft cheek, "good night, Dr. Harper."

She smiled; "good night, Mr. Roark."

CHAPTER 37

❀

England versus Azerbaijan

October 13, 2004, Baku Azerbaijan. Four days after their victory against Wales, England was ready to play Azerbaijan. Azerbaijan was a tough, gritty team that fought for everything they could get. From the starting whistle on, it was obvious Azerbaijan was going to be no push over. It was unmistakable by the electricity in the stands and from the hard fouls early on. In the first half, Azerbaijan did not have any serious goal scoring opportunities. However, England had many chances, but their inability to capitalize was apparent. England played sloppy football for forty-five minutes. Shots were missed, head balls misjudged. On more than several occasions, England forwards fell to Azerbaijan offside traps. The English offense was playing lousy, but the defense was playing its finest game to date. At halftime the score was deadlocked at zero.

Sir Robbie Kiel, sarcastically, "gentlemen, we are playing great. We are playing so well that after the game I am going to get everybody pay raises."

The locker room was calm. No one said a word. No one even looked at Robbie Kiel as he spoke. Kiel looked back at his troops and smiled.

Sir Robbie Kiel spoke again, "listen, guys. After this game we don't play another preliminary match until March of 2005. That is five months from now. Do you guys want to think about this lackluster effort for five months? I sure don't! I want to win now and be in control of our group. I do not wish to leave our hopes of winning the World Cup to chance."

The whole team nodded in agreement. The second half for England was a much better effort. It was crystal clear that England was the better team. They were bigger, stronger and much more talented than Azerbaijan. In the sixty-sixth minute, England struck. Walter Harrison received a long through ball from Brian Brazil, and he was off to the races. There was nobody in the Azerbaijan defense who could run with this speedster. Harrison got to the ball before anyone else as the Azerbaijan goalkeeper made an attempt to come out of the goal as quickly as he could. With one fast move, Harrison went around the goalkeeper and put the ball into the empty net. The English contingency in Baku became ecstatic. Harrison ran to the area where the English fans were seated and embraced their cheers while pointing at them with his index finger. England 1, Azerbaijan 0.

For the next thirty-two minutes, England played textbook style football. It was a football clinic England was demonstrating for Azerbaijan. Every loose ball, every fifty-fifty ball, was won by England. The effort level had gone up to new heights for England. After four games in the preliminaries, England had ten out of a possible twelve points. It was good enough for England to be tied for first place with Poland. England defeated Azerbaijan that evening in Baku and they were now in control of their own fate.

CHAPTER 38

† *Marriage*

A lot of things happened after the Azerbaijan match. Robbie Kiel and Katie Roark started dating. It was as if they hadn't missed a beat in twenty-three years. They were a couple in love. After dating for two weeks, Katie moved in with Robbie. Katie could not believe she had let this guy out of her life for all those years. During the night when Robbie slept next to her, she tried to get closer to him and hold him tighter. She never wanted to let him go again. Meanwhile, Robbie had work to do. He was still in charge of Manchester United and the team started off stronger than ever. Manchester won their first twelve games, and the fans were going crazy. They loved Robbie Kiel. Even the fans who wanted to hate Kiel and Manchester United were jumping on the bandwagon. After all, Kiel was English football. If he could make Manchester United play this well, he sure could take England over the hump for their second World Cup title with his wonder boy in goal.

Josh's personal life was going as well as his mother's and Robbie's. He had fallen for Lisa Harper. They spoke on the phone almost everyday, and Lisa came to England to see Josh as much as she could. She felt the same way about Josh as he did about her. She, too, was in love. December of 2004, Josh had new plans. He needed advice. He picked up the phone and called his confidant, Robbie Kiel. They made plans to meet at Robbie's place.

Robbie, seeing Josh, "how is my captain doing?"

Josh, smiling, "Coach, I am doing fine."

Robbie, "are you ready for football to resume after the holidays?"

Josh, "of course. I missed it so much. I am ready to win every match I play."

Robbie, "that is the right attitude."

Josh, "where is, Mother?"

Robbie, "she went grocery shopping."

Josh, "good. I needed to talk to you alone."

Robbie, a little worried, "what is wrong, Josh?"

Josh, "I am planning on asking Lisa to marry me on New Year's Eve."

Robbie, "that is fantastic!"

Josh, "how do I do it?"

Robbie, "do what?"

Josh, "how do I ask her to marry me?"

Robbie, "I don't know! I never asked anyone to marry me, either."

Josh, "but you know. You are older."

Robbie, "Josh, not that much older. I would probably get on my knee and be as romantic as possible. After all, she is going to remember this day for the rest of her life."

Josh, "do you think she is going to say yes?"

Robbie, "of course!"

Josh, "what makes you so sure?"

Robbie, "you are Josh Roark, the greatest goalie this country has seen. Every father of a daughter in England wants their daughter to marry you. People love you."

Josh, "thanks, Coach. This is helpful. It gives me confidence."

Robbie, "and one more thing."

Josh, "what is it?"

Robbie, "I know she is in love with you, too."

Josh, "how?"

Robbie, "I have seen the way she looks at you."

Josh, "thank you, Robbie."

Robbie, "no problem."

The door opened and Katie came in with some bags in her hands. Robbie jumped up out of his seat to help her.

Katie, "hello, my king. How are you?"

Josh hugged his mother; "I am doing fine. I missed you, Mother."

Katie, "you know where I live; you should come by more often. But I missed you, too."

Josh, "I stopped by to talked to you both."

Katie, "how is Lisa?"

Josh, "she is doing fine, flying back and forth."

Katie, "well, that is the problem with long distance relationships."

Josh, "I know."

Robbie smiled; "I am doing okay. I wanted to ask you something."

Josh, "what is it?"

Robbie, "it is a matter of the heart."

Josh, "what is it?"

Robbie, "do you mind if I ask your mother to marry me?"

Josh, stunned for a second, then smiled, "of course not. I love you, Robbie. I hope she says yes."

Robbie, "how should I do it?"

Josh, with a grin, "just like you told me. Get on your knees and ask. After all, you are Robbie Kiel. You are England's favorite son."

Robbie, "okay, I am ready."

Josh, "when are you going to do it?"

Robbie, "right now is as good a time as any."

Josh, "are you sure?"

Robbie, "yes, sir. Do I have your blessing?"

Josh hugged his hero; "of course you do."

Robbie and Josh left the room. They walked into the living room of Robbie's mansion. Katie was sitting down looking through a magazine. Robbie walked to Katie and gave her a kiss on the cheek. He knelt right next to her and opened the box.

Katie, panicked, "what are you doing?"

Robbie opened the box and grabbed the ring; "Katie, will you marry me?"

Josh was smiling the whole time Robbie was on his knees. This was the first time in his life he had seen his hero look vulnerable. His mother made eye contact with her grown son, and he just smiled back to her.

Katie looked at the ring and then looked at Robbie; "yes. I will marry you, Robbie Kiel."

Robbie stood up and so did Katie. They looked into each other's eyes and kissed. After they stopped kissing they turned and hugged Josh.

Josh, "this is amazing. That is the most romantic thing I have ever seen."

Robbie, "I guess you, too, know how to do it now."

Katie, "do what?"

Robbie, "he is going to ask Lisa to marry him."

Katie, smiling in joy, "I know she is going to say yes. I have seen the way Lisa looks at you, sweetheart. She looks at you the same way I look at Robbie."

CHAPTER 39

❀

† England versus Northern Ireland

March 26, 2005, Manchester England. England's opponent that day was Northern Ireland. In the past five months, things had changed drastically in both Robbie Kiel's and Josh Roark's lives. They both got engaged. They both moved in with their fiances. At the same time, they had not missed a beat with their work. Manchester continued winning., only dropping one match since the season had started.

England came out of the gates hard and fast against Northern Ireland. In the sixth minute, England's leading scorer, Walter Harrison, struck on a cross from young Bobby Wade, Harrison scored with a magnificent diving header. England 1, Northern Ireland 0. English fans were going mad. Five minutes later, in the eleventh minute, Walter Harrison struck again. He received a pass outside the box by Joel Johnson and went around one Northern Ireland defender. Without even looking at the goal, Harrison shot the ball as hard as he could. It was a low line drive that found the Northern Ireland net. England 2, Northern Ireland 0. For the rest of the first half, England played flawless football. At halftime Robbie Kiel was very happy with his team's performance.

> Sir Robbie Kiel, "unbelievable effort out there. Everyone is playing hard, and everyone is doing a wonderful job. You guys are playing like you want to win the cup. I am proud of you."

Everyone started clapping. Josh Roark raised his hand. Kiel saw this; "what is it, Roark?"

Josh, "can I say something, Coach?"

Sir Robbie Kiel, "your captain wishes to speak."

Josh turned to his teammates; "we haven't won shit. We only played one good half. Stop celebrating. Go back out there, and score two more goals. Go back out there, and play another flawless half. Than comeback and celebrate. No mental errors, team. Attention and execution make a perfect combination."

England went back and played another superb half. In the fifty-second minute, Brian Brazil scored on a beautiful bending free kick. The Northern Ireland goalkeeper stood stationary as the ball curved around the Northern Ireland wall and found the net. Old Trafford absolutely shook. England 3, Northern Ireland 0. England was not stopping, either. In the eighty-fourth minute, the young speedster from Liverpool, Walter Harrison, scored his third goal. On a counter attack Harrison took off from midfield against two defenders, and it was simply a foot race Northern Ireland defensive players could not win. Harrison took it to the house. England 4, Northern Ireland 0. Old Trafford was now in an uproar. The crowd stood up for the next few minutes and chanted for England. The chants turned into "win the cup."

CHAPTER 40

❀

† *England versus Azerbaijan*

March 30, 2005, Newcastle England. England was ready to play Azerbaijan for the second time.

> Before the game, Sir Robbie Kiel addressed his troops, "men, this is a big match. These guys played us hard in Baku. Now they are going to try to beat us at our home. I want everyone to remember, if you pay attention to detail and execute properly, we cannot lose. We are the best team in the world."

England had built a new reputation under Kiel's leadership. They were known around the world as a team of hooligans. On defense, Osley, Correal, Taggart and Landry were immensely talented with quick tempers. In midfield, Brazil, Laird, Johnson and Wade were known as the young guns of England. Laird and Wade were very physical players who had a reputation of playing dirty. Up front, Harrison and Cooper were equally dirty, living up to their team's reputation.

England's philosophy had become simple under Kiel. If the ball passes you, your opponent does not. That is how England played. They played hard, and they played to win. In the sixteenth minute against Azerbaijan, the Azerbaijan forward knocked into Roark hard on a corner kick. Taggart, Correal and Landry immediately went after the guy as if he had bumped them. The head referee gave a verbal warning to all of the parties involved in the altercation and let everyone know the next card coming out of his pocket would be red.

As Kiel watched his team's grittiness, he had become more convinced that his England team was much more united than any other team he had ever been a part of. Kiel's confidence about his team's chances for the World Cup grew by the second. In the forty-first minute of the first half, England's temperamental mid-fielder, Bobby Wade, scored on a penalty kick. England 1, Azerbaijan 0. The first half ended with England leading by one.

The physical play continued throughout the second half. England would not let their opponents claw back into the game. The English players knew any kind of backing off would send the wrong message to the rest of the world. In the fifty-third minute, Walter Harrison scored again. The goal resulted from plain and simple hustle. Brian Brazil went around an Azerbaijan player in the midfield then switched fields to Bobby Wade. Wade received the ball and switched it all the way forward to Harrison. Azerbaijan players thought the ball was going out so they slowed down. But Harrison had the speed of a world-class sprinter. He chased the ball down, caught up with it and went straight to the Azerbaijan goal. With no angle he blasted a shot at the goalkeeper. As the goalkeeper reacted to the ball, it went between his legs into the Azerbaijan net. England 2, Azerbaijan 0. St. James Park was officially going insane just as Old Trafford had in the previous national team matches.

England beat Azerbaijan in Newcastle that evening two to zero. England now had won five straight matches, and they were still the odds on favorite to win their group to advance to Germany.

> After the game, Kiel spoke, "men, I am proud of you. That is five straight now. We will continue winning no matter who we play. We are going to be the champions of the world."

Everybody in the locker room, including the water boys, clapped like maniacs. Kiel had pumped everyone up again. He was known to be a master speaker and an amazing motivator. Kiel's and his captain's reputations in England and around the world were growing in the blink of an eye.

CHAPTER 41

❦

† Success

By the time June 10, 2006 rolled around, things had changed in Josh Roark's life. He had gotten married to Lisa earlier that month. By the following year, Lisa had their first child. Lisa and Josh named their son Bobby Charlton Roark. Josh had never been this happy in his entire life. Being a father made him feel special about himself. His life was perfect. In the meantime, Robbie Kiel and Katie Roark had tied the knot in 2005 as well. Katie Roark had officially become Mrs. Robbie Kiel after twenty-five years.

On the football front, England won the rest of their preliminary matches. In September of 2005, England beat Wales in Wales four to one. Then four days later, England spanked Northern Ireland two to zero behind a magnificent goalkeeper display by Josh Roark. England was on cruise control. They had not been this dominant in the past twenty years.

The following month, England's supremacy in their group was indisputable. They beat Austria in Old Trafford five to zero. The rest of the world had taken notice of the whipping of the Austrian national team. Four days later, on October 12, England beat Poland in a mesmerizing way. England had won the game in St. James Park two to zero.

England had officially qualified for World Cup Germany. England qualified with twenty-eight points, one of the highest point totals from any team that had qualified to the Cup ever. The British Kingdom was ready for England to return back to the glory days of English football. They were ready to win like they did in the Charlton era. Forty years later, another true star would emerge for England on football's grandest stage. With some help from his own childhood hero, captain Roark was ready to capture his own destiny and the imagination of England. The Three Lions were ready to roar again. England was ready to win.

CHAPTER 42

† *Group B*

England made it to Germany ten days before the World Cup started. Robbie Kiel became worried once he found out what group England was in and who else was in the same group with them. England was put in Group B with Japan, Spain and Turkey. All three of these teams had participated in World Cup Japan/Korea 2002.

Reporters in Germany were dying for a headline; "Sir Robbie, what do you think about your group?"

Sir Robbie Kiel, "I think our group is probably the hardest of all the other groups in this tournament."

Reporter, "why is that, sir?"

Kiel looked at the reporter with a smirk; "let me draw you a map. We have Turkey in our group. As you know, they finished number three in 2002. They have an even better team now. They are fast and strong. Their center forward, Bulut Ozturk led Inter in scoring in the past two years. After Turkey, we have Japan. They have those working twin bees in the middle."

Reporter, "I believe you are referring to the Nishimura twins."

Kiel, with sarcasm, "who else would I refer to on that team as twins? Haruka and Haruki Nishimura are probably the best one-two combination in this World Cup."

Reporter, "better than your two mid-fielder combination of Brian Brazil and Jason Laird?"

Kiel smiled; "of course. My boys are always inconsistent."

Reporter, "are the Nishimura twins better than the Wade and Johnson combination?"

Kiel, aggravated, "if they weren't, I wouldn't say they were, would I?"

Reporter, "what about Spain?"

Kiel, "as you know, they are always one of the best teams in the world. They are unbelievably scary, especially up in the forward area. I know you have seen Emillio Pantagosa in action. He is super."

Reporter, "is England ready for this tournament?"

Kiel, "we are as ready as we can be; however, we are stuck in a group with the scariest teams in the world."

CHAPTER 43

❀

† Group B: England versus Japan

Saturday, June 10. England would play their first match at Westfalenstadion in Dortmund, Germany. After warming up on the field for forty-five minutes, England went back into their locker room. The players were nervous, the coaches as well. Robbie Kiel walked over his footsteps for five minutes or so before speaking.

Coach Kiel, "all of my life, as long as I can remember, I wanted to be a football player. When I became a football player all I cared about was winning for my country. I came close several times in World Cups, and it always broke my heart when I failed. I want you to know now, that this experience of playing in this World Cup for your country is going to go by in a blink of an eye. Days are going to fly by, and time will be in fast forward. Enjoy the game of football, and enjoy this experience. If you don't, you will be an old washed up has-been like myself, talking about the good old days of English football."

Everybody in the English locker room had this intense look on their faces. Robbie Kiel looked around the room and made eye contact with each one of his starters.

Kiel called, "Walter Harrison?"

Harrison replied, "yes, sir!"

Kiel, "are you ready to win the World Cup?"

Harrison shouted, "yes, sir!"

Kiel, "Jeremy Cooper?"

Cooper, "yes, sir!"

Kiel, "are you ready?"

Cooper, like Harrison, shouted, "yes, sir!"

Kiel looked around the room and found his stopper, Martin Taggart; "Taggart, are you ready?"

Taggart shouted back, "yes, sir!"

Kiel looked around and found his sweeper, Adam Osley; "are you ready, Osley?"

Osley, "yes, sir!"

As Kiel went through the room, staring at each player and asking his question, all the Lions started standing up. Kiel looked around and found the most intense face in the room besides his.

Kiel looked at England's captain then shouted his name; "Roark, are you ready to capture what is yours?"

Roark declared back in a clear tone, "I have been waiting my whole life for this moment. We will win. We will win. We will win."

The whole locker room echoed with those three words, "we will win." The players started clapping in unison and then all put their right index fingers up in the air. The whole team screamed as one, "England".

At 1500 hours, England erupted onto the field to play in front of a full capacity of 60,000 fans in Westfalenstadion. The game against Japan started quickly for both teams. As the teams came emerged from the gates, it was obvious both sides had their hearts on scoring first. In the seventh minute, England caught a break. On a long pass from Bobby Wade, Walter Harrison started running as the ball was kicked. The Japanese defense stood still and raised their hands up to signal off-sides. The head referee looked at the sideline referee for his flag to go up, but it did not. The flag never went up, therefore the head referee did not blow his whistle and let the play continue. Harrison got to the ball, and the Japanese goalkeeper came out of his goal in disbelief. He could not believe the referee had missed such a clear call. The Japanese goalkeeper made a lackluster move towards Harrison, but his efforts were a little too late. Harrison chipped the ball over the sliding Japanese goalkeeper, and England had officially gone up one to zero. The English crowd at Dortmund was going wild.

In the next fifteen minutes Japan attacked relentlessly. The Nishimura twins were like the energizer bunny. They were all over the field. England's best answer against to these two spectacular players was to play physical football with them in an attempt to wear them out. In the twenty-third minute, in England's box, Haruka Nishimura made one quick move and went around John Landry. As soon as Nishimura went around Landry, he found a roadblock in Derrick Correal. Correal, like he had been trained, fouled Nishimura hard in England's penalty box. The head referee would not blow two calls in a row. He immediately blew his whistle and pointed at the penalty spot. Then he went into his left pocket and took out one of his cards. He went up to Correal and gave him a red card. The England mid-fielders and defenders argued with the referee as he pointed at the spot.

> Captain Roark was trying to reason with the head referee from Sweden, "sir, he was going for the ball. That whole play was all ball, sir. He did not deserve a red card for that innocent touch."

The referee did not respond. He stood over the penalty spot and cleared all the English players out of the area. Haruka Nishimura, the younger twin by two minutes, was ready to take the kick. He went back, then came up to the ball with his left foot and put the ball in the upper ninety. England 1, Japan 1. The Japanese spectators in Dortmund came alive.

After Correal's ejection, the game took a different turn. With the right side of the defense one player short, Roark pulled Brazil back to defense. The next fifteen minutes Japan continued invading the English territory. One man short, Japan dominated England. Japan super fast and they were spreading the field very well against England. Japan was taking full advantage of being one man up against the Three Lions. In the forty-third minute, Japan's relentless efforts were answered again. On a counter attack, Japan caught England with only two players back in defense. Landry and Brazil had gone up to offense for a corner kick in the previous possession. As a result, Japan had taken full advantage of this opportunity and countered quickly. Both of those players could not get back in time to their respective positions. Haruka Nishimura sent a smooth long ball to his twin, Haruki. Upon receiving the ball, Haruki did a scissor motion over the ball as he dribbled towards Taggart, completely fooling the English stopper as if he was a defenseless little kid. After going around Taggart, he saw Roark charging out of the goal. Haruki cocked his foot and nailed a shot between Roark's sliding legs into the English net. Japan 2, England 1. The first half ended with England down by one and the Japanese crowd in a frenzy. Life had been sucked out of the English crowd.

Coach Kiel, in the locker room, "guys, what are we doing wrong?"

No one answered.

Coach Kiel, "we are one player down, and they are taking advantage of our mistakes. We have to start paying attention to little details. Those two little kids are taking you to school. My defensive players, start thinking about what you are doing on defense. My mid-fielders, start thinking like a World Cup team. My forwards, I need more out of you. Get your heads out of your asses. Let's go and get back in this match."

The locker room was silent as ever. Everyone looked at the ground as if they had already been defeated.

Coach Kiel, unhappy with the mood of the team, started shouting again, "listen to me, you little arrogant fucks. There isn't a single good footballer in this room. You guys are bunch of sorry-ass, overpaid athletes. In my opinion, this team has no heart and no character. Look at you looking at the floor. What the fuck is wrong with you people? You played one half in the World Cup and you act like it is the end of the world. Fucking unbelievable!"

Captain Roark all of a sudden snapped in frustration with his coach and shouted at him; "there is nothing wrong with us. We are not scared, and we are not going to lose this game. I want you to tell me what the hell you want from my team and me. Give us direction, and tell us what you want us to do. Quit bitching for a change!"

Kiel started shouting back at Roark; "you can't lead properly, Roark. Your team does not want to follow you. Take off that fucking captain armband. You are the biggest mistake I ever made thus far."

Roark started shouting harder at Kiel, pointing at him as he yelled; "this is my team! You have to kill me to take this captain armband off of me, you stubborn bastard!"

The players tried to hold both Roark and Kiel back as tempers flared. Kiel looked at Roark and made one more comment; "you are the worst goalie in this World Cup, remember that."

With that comment, Kiel slammed the locker room door and walked out. Kiel started heading back to the field. As he walked, he smiled from head to toe as if he had fallen in love once again. He knew he did not have to say anything else to the team. Roark would take care his team. Roark had officially been pissed off. He was just like him. He would play better being angry. Kiel knew Roark would make the necessary adjustments that he himself would have made and would play for the win. He would inspire his teammates in the locker room, and they would follow.

Roark, still angry in the locker room began throwing chairs against the wall, going absolutely ballistic. He ripped off whatever suits he could find, and thrashed the locker room in the next two minutes.

Roark screamed at his teammates, "wake up! If you don't want to win, why didn't you stay back in England?! I don't care if we are down one player; we are still going to win this game. I want all your energy now, and then you people can rest for two days. Let's go out there and play English football."

It was instilled in Josh Roark's blood not to go for the tie. He would go for the win regardless of the situation. He was the ultimate leader. His teammates would follow him anywhere and do anything for him. They did not want to disappoint their captain who always took all the blame.

In the second half, one man down, England made their adjustments. England had Roark in goal. Roark had decided they would play 3-4-2. Landry, Osley and Taggart played defense. Brazil, Wade, Laird and Johnson would play midfield. Up front, Walter Harrison and Jeremy Cooper played forwards. The second half was nothing like the first. England played intensity-ridden super football. Every loose ball and every head ball was won by the bigger and stronger English team. Every time the Nishimura twins touched the ball, they would be punished for their attempts by a much more physical English team. Brian Brazil received a yellow card in the sixtieth minute for fouling Haruka Nishimura in dangerous fashion. In the seventy third minute, the same yellow card came out for Bobby Wade. It was for the same offense, but to the other Nishimura brother. England's message to the twins was clear; you touch the ball, you get punished. Even with intensity on England's side, England still had not scored.

In the eightieth minute, England finally scored a goal. On an England corner kick, Roark emptied out his backfield. He sent everybody up forward, including his two six feet three tall defenders, Martin Taggart and Adam Osley. Strategy wise, this was an excellent move. These two defenders were the tallest guys on the field. They would have height advantage over the smaller Japanese defenders. Bobby Wade took the kick from the right corner flag and Taggart went up for it. As Taggart went up higher for the ball, all of a sudden, someone else had gotten up just a notch higher than him. The ball had found the back of the Japanese net. Taggart had not seen what had just transpired. Taggart surely thought he had that header. By the time Taggart realized what happened, Osley had scored and ran towards the English crowd, pointing at his heart. The English crowd was officially back in the game. England 2, Japan 2. For the next ten minutes England attacked and attacked some more. They were on a mission. The English crowd was doing everything in their power to help their team. They stood up and chanted with all their heart for the next ten minutes. In the ninetieth minute, the fourth referee from the sideline had lifted a sign that said three more minutes of additional time. To Japan, those three minutes seemed like forever. England attacked, and, finally, in the ninety-second minute, their prayers were answered. England had scored on an amazing shot from Jason Laird. He received the ball thirty-eight yards out from the Japanese goal, and, with all his might, nailed a shot into the Japanese goal. It was as if the ball was a missile and the football gods guided the ball into the upper ninety of the Japanese net. Suddenly, the English crowd erupted. England had done it. They had come back from being one player and one goal down to take a lead on Japan, three to two. Japan tried to get back to the midfield as quickly as possible to restart the game. Five seconds later the game was over. England 3, Japan 2.

In the English locker room there were total jubilation. Kiel raised his hand up in the air and said, "congratulations, men. You have won your first World Cup match. I am proud of you. But we have to win six more of these to win in order for us to get the World Cup."

Everyone stopped laughing and clapping. They had become silent again seeing that Kiel had more to say.

Kiel, "gentlemen, the game ball goes to our fearless leader, your captain, Josh Roark."

The entire locker room erupted once again. Celebration had begun. The fans of England were amazed. England had shown amazing heart with one man down and won against a tough Japanese team. After the game, English reporters were everywhere during the news conferences.

A Japanese reporter, Laura Taketa, asked Coach Kiel, "Sir Kiel, what did you say to your men at halftime?"

Kiel smiled and looked at the camera; "I just told them to follow their captain."

Ms. Taketa, puzzled, "is that it?"

Kiel smiled again; "that is it!"

Five hours earlier in Frankfurt, Turkey had beaten Spain one to zero behind Bulut Ozturk's penalty kick. Turkey and England were tied for first place. Spain and Japan were tied for second.

❀

CHAPTER 44

† *Group B: England versus Spain*

Thursday, June 15, 2006. At 1800 hours England would play Spain. The game in Nuremberg started off slowly. Both teams realized the importance of the game and played cautious football for the first forty-five minutes. England knew that with a win they would guarantee themselves a spot in the round of sixteen, but with a defeat they would let everyone else in their group back into contention. England versus Spain was a very boring match for the first seventy minutes. No real chances presented themselves for either side. However, in the last twenty minutes of the match, the game became more exciting. In the seventy-eighth minute, Derrick Correal's replacement, Patrick Mason, committed a handball in the England penalty area. It was unintentional usage of the hands but the referee from the United States immediately blew the whistle and awarded Spain with a penalty kick. English players argued the call with the referee as the fans booed the call. The Spaniard star, Emillio Pantagosa, lined up and took a hard shot to the left side of the goal with his right foot. Roark guessed the correct spot and, in one motion, punched the ball out of bounds. The English fans clapped and screamed as if they had already won the World Cup. They were vindicated for the horrible call made by the American referee. However, Spain still had a corner kick. On the following Spanish corner kick, Spain had another excellent chance with Pantagoso's header. But the English captain was there again to make another huge save.

In the eighty-fifth minute, England decided to attack. English attackers came from all corners. The mid-fielders pushed forward as well as the defenders. Four minutes later, in the eighty-ninth minute, England came down from the left side of the field. With a couple of quick passes between Wade and Cooper, England suddenly found an opening in the Spanish defense. Cooper dribbled in as fast as he could from the left side into the box and found streaking Brian Brazil by the penalty area. Brazil one touched the ball past the Spanish goalkeeper, England 1, Spain 0. As soon as Brazil scored, he ran towards his own sideline and celebrated with the rest of his team. English fans in Frankenstadion cheered in a happy hysteria. The English contingency was in a joyous mood. In the next few minutes, England played tight defense and won for the second time in as many games in Germany.

> After the game, Kiel spoke to his troops; "men, I am proud of you. We have five more games to go in order to accomplish our goal. I have a game ball here for the man who scored the winning goal, Brian Brazil."

All the players in the locker room shouted Brazil's name. Brazil raised his hands up in the air to quiet the room.

> Kiel, "Brazil has something he wants to say."

> Brazil lifted his ball up high and said, "this ball belongs to our Captain. If it wasn't for many of his great saves today, there is no way I would have scored that goal. Thank you for inspiring me."

> Roark walked up to Brazil, gave him a hug and lifted the ball up in the air and shouted to his teammates; "five more wins to go."

The English locker room continued in celebration. That night, elsewhere in Germany, the Turkish superstar, Bulut Ozturk, carried Turkey to their second victory in as many games. Ozturk scored both of his country's goals against Japan. He had officially become the leading goal scorer in the World Cup. His second goal against Japan was probably one of the best goals of all time. On a cross Ozturk had scored in Pele-like fashion with an amazing bicycle kick. Olympiastadion in Berlin had never before been that loud. Seventy-six thousand fans stood up and gave the Turkish maestro a standing ovation that lasted almost a minute. No Turkish player had ever seen this kind of ovation in Berlin until that night.

Group B was deadlocked at the top. England and Turkey would advance to the round of sixteen. But they both had one more game left against each other. This would be a clash of the titans for group supremacy.

CHAPTER 45

❁

† Group B: England versus Turkey

Mr. Thacker, "what do you think about your upcoming match against Turkey?"

Sir Robbie Kiel, "I don't know, Mr. Thacker. They are a very strong team.

Slowly they are becoming fan favorites here. Bulut Ozturk is something else. He is playing at a different level than everyone else in this tournament. It is going to be tough. We have to play our best game to beat Turkey."

Mr. Thacker, "are you worried?"

Sir Robbie Kiel, "of course, I am. I figured we go only as far as Josh Roark takes us in this tournament. If he plays well, we will win. If not, we will go home!"

Mr. Thacker, "aren't you being a little too hard on your captain?"

Kiel looked into Mr. Thacker's eyes with all the conviction in the world; "absolutely not."

June 20, 2006, Kaiserslautern, Germany, 2100 hours. The England versus Turkey match was one of the hottest tickets in Germany. England had played Turkey in a friendly game two years earlier in Istanbul. Turkey had beat England on that day, two to one, without their superstar forward, Bulut

Ozturk. After the match, English fans had gotten into a fight with bunch of Turkish fans that resulted in the arrests of more than fifty people. Much bad blood existed between these two countries's teams and their fans. Lines were drawn and security in Kaiserslautern would be extra tight on this evening.

As the game started, it was apparent neither team was going to make a mistake that would cost them the match. Both teams made short, sure passes that did not lead to major mistakes. England, as well as Turkey, was playing conservative football. With the exception of a foul here and a foul there the game was too slow for both countries' fans. Every time Bulut Ozturk touched the ball, the English fans would boo the Turkish superstar. In return, Turkish fans booed England's most beloved player, Josh Roark, every time he touched the ball. Despite the slow play, the first half went rather quickly. Throughout the first half, England always had somebody keeping an eye on Ozturk's every move. England's strategy was clear; they wouldn't let Ozturk beat them. Anyone else could try to beat them from Turkey, but Ozturk wouldn't be the one who beat them that day. The first half ended with both teams tied at zero.

The second half at Fritz-Walter-Stadion was more of the same, slow boring football. Both sides simply played not to lose. In the fifty-third minute, Turkey received a controversial call outside the eighteen. Bulut Ozturk went around two English defenders and seemed to take a dive right outside the box. As soon as he went down, the referee blew the whistle and awarded a free kick for Turkey. The English players argued the call, but the referee would not change his mind. Even the replays on the stadium televisions showed Ozturk had amazing acting potential that may someday lead him to Hollywood. This left-footed sensation would take the free kick. He lined up and bent a shot around the wall past the diving English goalkeeper's arms. At the last second, Roark was able to get a hand on the ball to alter its trajectory over the top of his own goal. It was a beautiful shot by Ozturk. Against any other goalie in the world that shot would have gone in. But Josh Roark was the best in the game. He would not be fooled in a game of this magnitude.

From the sixty minute mark on, both teams raised their level of play. They started playing at a faster pace. Both teams began attacking. First Turkey started taking shots from anywhere and everywhere. They weren't real threats, but it kept Roark busy. In return, England attacked with six, seven or sometimes even eight players at a time. They sent boatloads of people up front to attempt to score. In the eighty-first minute, England executed a perfect attack that originated from the right side of the midfield. Brian Brazil started the attack by switching fields to Bobby Wade. There, Wade trapped the ball and sent it back to the middle to the oncoming Jason Laird. Laird was in the middle of the field and saw Walter Harrison making a run towards the left side of the eighteen. With that, he sent a quick pass that led Harrison to the left corner flag. Harrison, at the corner flag, saw the Turkish defender closing the gap towards him and sent a cross into the Turkish penalty area. There, the ball found the feet of the person who had started this whole attack. Brian Brazil saw the cross from Walter Harrison and moved towards the ball. Without hesitation, Brazil one touched the ball into the back of the Turkish net. England 1, Turkey 0. Brian Brazil ran with his hands in the air to the corner flag. He made the motion of holding a baby in his hands as if he was trying to put it to sleep. The English fans in Fritz-Walter-Stadion loved this display of showmanship. They clapped and screamed as loud as possible.

Pandemonium was everywhere.

England went on to hold off the late charge of the Turkish national team. They prevailed over Turkey. After the game, the English reporters could not wait to interview Sir Robbie Kiel. Of course, the exclusive interview would go to Kiel's favorite journalist, William Thacker.

Mr. Thacker, "Sir Robbie Kiel, what adjustments did you make in the second half?"

Robbie Kiel, "Mr. Thacker, I really did not make any changes at all. I just told the boys, let's go for the win. We don't play for a tie. My team knows I would rather lose than tie."

Thacker, "what do you think about your chances in the next round?"

Robbie, "I think we have as good of a chance as the other fifteen teams."

Mr. Thacker, "can you win the whole thing?"

Robbie, "that all depends on our captain."

Mr. Thacker, "what do you mean?"

Robbie, "as I said before, if it was not for Josh Roark, we would not be here today. If he goes, England goes."

Mr. Thacker, "don't you think that is a lot of pressure on that young guy?"

Robbie, "you asked that same question after our last game, Mr. Thacker. Let me explain something to you, sir, pressure is something you feel when you don't know what the hell you are doing. Our captain does not feel pressure. He does not even know what that word means. He is the most prepared person that I have ever met."

CHAPTER 46

❀

† Player Coach Meeting

England had five days off before their next game against their arch-rival, Argentina, in the round of sixteen. Robbie Kiel asked to meet with his goal-keeper in his hotel room.

Kiel, "Josh, how are you?"

Josh, "I am doing fine. How are you?"

Kiel, "I am worried about you."

Josh, surprised, "why, Coach?"

Kiel, "have I put too much pressure on you?"

Josh smiled; "no, sir! Never! I know you are one of those coaches who likes to play mind games. I like that. It keeps all of us on our toes."

Kiel, "are you sure I haven't put too much pressure on you?"

Josh smiled again; "no, Coach. What do I have to do to prove it to you?"

Kiel smiled; "you can prove it to me by bringing England the World Cup."

Josh, with all the seriousness in the world, looked at Kiel; "I will take care of that."

Kiel, "how is your son?"

Josh smiled; "young Bobby is doing well."

Kiel, "how is Lisa?"

Josh, "she is okay."

Kiel, "don't worry, two more weeks and it is all over with. We will be the champions of the world."

Josh, "four more wins."

❀

CHAPTER 47

† Round of Sixteen: England versus Argentina

Round of sixteen, Gottlieb-Daimler-Stadion, Stuttgart. England versus Argen-tina was one of the most anticipated matches in the round of sixteen. These two rivals never hated each other more until that June evening. The winner would move forward to the quarter-finals of the World Cup, and the loser would go back to their country in shame. This game was the right for both teams to continue dreaming. For the winner, the dream of being champion would still be present. The loser of the Argentina England match would have to wait another four years for their chance to dream of winning the cup again. The bragging rights would belong to the winner of this clash for four more years. This game was big. This was a championship in and of itself between these two thunderous football nations.

England's game versus Argentina started at 1700 hours. As soon as the whistle for the beginning of the game was blown, it was clear that both sides at Gottlieb-Daimler-Stadion were ready to play their best football. Argentina started the game strongly with their superstar forwards. In the seventh minute, Argentina had the game's first real chance of scoring. Outside of England's box, the Argentine international had taken a shot that went past the outstretched arms of Josh Roark and ricocheted off the crossbar. The English fans, Robbie Kiel, Josh Roark and the rest of the English team breathed a collective sigh of relief. In the twelfth minute, England came back with their own attempt at a point. Walter Harrison started an attack in the middle of the field. He dribbled for a second and saw John Landry making a run from his left fullback position. Harrison quickly made a pass to streaking Landry, where, upon receiving the ball, Landry made a one touch cross to the penalty area. There, Bobby Wade jumped into the air and headed the ball perfectly. However, at the last second, the Argentine goalkeeper was able to get his hand on the ball to send it over the goal.

The first half of the England versus Argentina match was a back and forward, intensity filled competition. Neither team made mistakes. Both teams were prepared to play at the highest level for the rest of the game. Their level of football was the best World Cup Germany had seen thus far. The first half ended in a scoreless tie. Both nations' fans stood up and applauded their respective teams as they went into their locker rooms.

> Robbie Kiel, at halftime, "gentlemen, we are playing excellent football. I am proud of everyone in this room for bringing your best game to this huge match. You people are true professionals. However, as you know, we are playing to win this match and move on to the next round. I want everyone to remember, attention and execution make a perfect combination. We have to turn it up one more notch."

The second half of the magnificent game was more of the same, amazing football on the world's biggest stage. In the sixtieth minute, England had their second great opportunity to score. This time, Derrick Correal, from his right fullback position, made an amazing run. Brian Brazil passed the ball to Correal. Correal stood over the ball for a second and made a short, sure pass to Bobby Wade at midfield. Wade made two moves in an attempt to juke the defender, but he could not get away from his Argentine national. He made a pass to Taggart. Taggart started running with the ball right down the middle of the field, unmarked. When he reached the twenty-five yard line, he blasted a right-footed shot. The ball took off like a cruise missile, slowly rising as it got closer to the goal. The Argentine goalkeeper made a move for it, but it was too late. The ball, with all its speed, hit the crossbar and went out of bounds. The English fans clapped hard. They knew this was not the same English team that had choked years earlier. In the seventy-third minute, the long-haired, flamboyant Argentine striker managed to sneak behind the English defense. He took a hard shot to the left side of the goal. Roark made another amazing save with his superb quickness. Argentine fans bemoaned the missed opportunity while the English fans applauded their captain's magnificent save.

For ninety minutes, England and Argentina played a scoreless game. The referee blew his whistle to end regulation time. It was only fitting that a game of this magnitude would go into overtime. The fans were getting all of their money's worth. In the first fifteen minutes of overtime nothing happened. Both teams were cautious with everything they did. One goal from either team would force the other team to pack their bags and go home. Naturally, neither team was willing to take this chance. The first overtime came to an end. The teams switched sides, and the game resumed. The intensity level for the amazing match had rubbed off to 60,000 plus fans. They did not stop cheering for their country that evening. Every touch, every call, every throw would be magnified and remembered for years to come. Robbie Kiel sat motionless on his bench as his team fought and clawed their way for an opportunity to move forward in the World Cup. In the 118th minute, England had another chance. Jeremy Cooper had the ball on the left side of the Argentina box. Instead of crossing the ball into the penalty area to his wide-open teammates, Cooper did the selfish thing and blasted a shot towards the Argentina goal. The ball went straight at one of the Argentina defender's leg and ricocheted into the Argentina net. The Argentina goalkeeper tried to reach for the ball, but it had taken a totally different direction than what he anticipated.

England had done it again. They had beaten Argentina two World Cups in a row. The match was over. England had won with a golden goal. England would now move into the quarter-finals. England and its fans celebrated their amazing victory over their arch-rival like they had won the World Cup for the next two nights. The bars in England had been prospering thanks to the successful run by the England National Team.

After the game, journalists everywhere asked the same question, "Sir Robbie Kiel, how did England pull this one out?"

Sir Robbie Kiel smiled; "too bad someone had to lose. Both teams played outstanding all the way to the very end. We were lucky. The ball rolled our way. I would like to take my hat off to Argentina and give them all the credit in the world for being one of the premier football nations in the world."

Reporter, Laura Taketa, managed to sneak in a question, "what are you feeling right now, Coach?"

Robbie Kiel had done interviews with Ms. Taketa before in London. She had become a prominent football writer for one of the premier newspapers in England.

Kiel smiled; "hello, Ms. Taketa, how are you?"

Laura Taketa, "I am doing fine, sir. I am happy that England prevailed."

Kiel, "me, too, Laura. Me too. I don't know what is going on, but I guess the football gods are on our side."

Laura, "what were you thinking as Jeremy Cooper took that shot?"

Kiel, "I thought it was one of the dumbest ideas anyone has ever had. He had no angle. He had two of our guys wide open in the middle. Instead, he chose to shoot."

Laura, "Are you ready for your next opponent?"

Kiel, "I would like to enjoy this win for another two hours or so and then go back to the drawing board."

Laura, "thank you, Coach."

Meanwhile, in the locker room, the game's hero was being interview by William Thacker.

Mr. Thacker, "Jeremy, how does it feel to be a hero?"

Cooper, "I don't know sir! I don't think I was the hero. I got lucky."

Mr. Thacker, "you are a hero in England now. They will play this shot over and over for years to come."

Jeremy Cooper smiled; "I got lucky, sir. I just hope we keep on winning."

The next morning in England, the newspapers read, "Kiel Says Football Gods Are With England."

CHAPTER 48

❀

† Quarter Finals: England versus United States

England had five days before their quarter-finals appearance in Gelsenkirchen against the United States. After England's win over Argentina, Robbie Kiel had arranged for the team to be off for two straight days. He had told the team that curfew was still in affect. He also told his troops to be responsible and rest during those two days. With those comments from the English skipper, Josh Roark had taken over and arranged team movies for the whole squad both days. Many in England questioned Kiel's decision of giving his team two days off. Football pundits disapproved of this decision in the middle of the World Cup.

William Thacker, "Sir Robbie, I know you hear the whispers in England."

Robbie replied, "yes, I do."

Mr. Thacker, "why would you give your team two days off at this stage of the World Cup?"

Robbie, "we played an emotional game against Argentina, and I wanted them to forget about that game. I want my team to relax to play against the United States."

Mr. Thacker, "this is the first time any coach has ever done this. Are you giving your players too much freedom?"

Robbie smiled; "they are all adults. They are all professionals. They all know our purpose."

Mr. Thacker, "what do you think about your chances against theUnited States?"

Robbie, "they are a strong team at all positions. We will try to keep up with them as much as possible."

Mr. Thacker, "thank you for the interview, Robbie."

Those five days flew by, and the scene was set at Arena AufSchalke, which held close to 53,000 fans. The English fans outnumbered the American fans by at least 10,000. England was ready to play. The match against the Americans started at 1700 hours. The Three Lions started the game stronger than ever. Once again, they were clicking on all cylinders. In the fifth minute, Walter Harrison missed a shot wide to the right. In the eighth minute, England missed another opportunity on a shot that sailed over the American goal. England was attacking from many different areas with many different guys. English defenders were making run after run. To the United States, it seemed like the whole British Kingdom was attacking in the first half. In the twenty-eighth minute, England got on the board first. Brian Brazil of England scored on one of the prettiest bending free kicks from twenty-two yards out. The American goalkeeper stood helpless as the ball bent over the wall and found the American net. Brazil raised his hands up pointing at the English fans and celebrated with the rest of his teammates. The English fans were going crazy. This was their team. England 1, America 0.

Ten minutes later, in the thirty-eighth minute, Walter Harrison got free on the right side of the field. He started dribbling straight down the touchline to the corner flag. As he got closer to the American box, he made a cross onto the six yard line. The ball came in on a perfect spin, and Bobby Wade volleyed the ball into the American goal. England was now up by two. England 2, United States 0. It was official, with the second goal by England, Arena AufSchalke had become England's. The English fans were experiencing excitement on a whole new level. The game had become no contest by the end of first half. The match versus the United States had become a home game for England. All of a sudden, the English players felt as if they were playing in Old Trafford.

At halftime, Kiel spoke, "gentlemen, I am proud of the football you are displaying. Your talents and skills are impressive. However, we have to play ninety minutes of intense football. We have to give our opponent ninety minutes of hell. Now listen up carefully, we will go out for the next forty-five minutes and dominate these American assholes like they have never been dominated before. We will send a message to the rest of the teams left here. We will let the world know that we are the best and we will win the cup."

The second half started the same way it ended. The Americans were clearly outclassed by England. And not only that, but they were out-hustled with every ball. In the fifty-third minute, Martin Taggart joined the goal scoring festivities with a head ball during a corner kick. Taggart had gone up front to use his immense size. This time he was successfully rewarded with a goal. England 3, United States 0. For the next thirty-seven minutes, England did not hold back any punches. While the English fans chanted, sang and just went crazy, England attacked and attacked some more. They attacked until they had beaten the Americans into submission. With their dominating performance, England would move into the semifinals of the World Cup.

After the game Kiel, addressed his troops; "gentlemen, this team inspires me. I am proud to be English, and I am proud to be your coach. I only have three words to say to you. Two more wins."

The next morning, all of England was buzzing with excitement. Before the World Cup started, everybody in England knew they had a strong team, but they thought in the back of their minds that this team would choke like the other teams of the past. Kiel was determined to get the job done. So was the rest of England! They hadn't seem a winner in forty years, and they were hungry for a title.

CHAPTER 49

❀

† Semi Finals: England versus Brazil

June 5, 2006, Munich Germany. England's opponent for the semifinal game ended up being the defending World Cup champion, Brazil. The setting was Stadion Munchen, capacity 66,000 people. Brazil had eliminated England in the last World Cup. They had been the best in the world for years. Was England ready?

England started off skittish against Brazil. They were making mistakes all over the place. They were missing passes. They were playing poorly. England was not ready for this challenge. Brazil, from the starting whistle, came out ready to play. England was shocked. They did not know what they were doing, and they were being beaten on every hustle. Everything started going Brazil's way. They were getting the bounces and the calls. The Three Lions were frustrated. Meanwhile, the Brazilian national team felt England's frustration. The defending champion of the world smelled blood. They could tell England was afraid, and they played off of it. They started attacking harder and harder. They took shots from every possible direction. But Josh Roark was ready once again. He was diving to his left saving shots, diving to his right saving shots. He had become the Great Wall of China covering his goal.

In the twentieth minute, the famous Brazilian striker had broken loose past the English defense was one-on-one with the English goalkeeper. As Roark began sliding sideways to close his angle, the Brazilian striker blasted a shot at Roark. The ball traveled at an amazing velocity, hit Roark's rock hard stomach and bounced all the way back to the midfield line. Roark jumped up from the ground immediately and raised his hands to his crowd to let them know he was here to play. The English spectators at Stadion Munchen appreciated this Rocky-like courage of Josh Roark. They responded with a standing ovation. The English fans started chanting, screaming and clapping harder than ever. The atmosphere in Stadion Munchen had suddenly become pro-England with one amazing save.

The English football team was inspired by their captain's play as well. Josh Roark had managed to wake up the English fans and the Lions with a single play. His will to win was contagious to everyone in the stadium. Every time England made a pass, the crowd screamed "oley!" England had found their stride. They started putting together several different combinations of passes in the midfield area, Brazil to Laird, Laird to Johnson, and than Johnson back to Brian Brazil. England now controlled the midfield and the game. In the thirty-second minute, Bobby Wade found Martin Taggart as he was making his run forward. Taggart one touched the ball to Brian Brazil and continued running down the left sideline. Brian Brazil did what he was supposed to do and sent a perfect high ball to the corner flag. Taggart, with his speed, got to the ball before it went out of bounds. He controlled the ball and made a quick move to his right to give himself an angle to cross the ball. With that angle, he laid a beautiful ball to the Brazilian ten yard line. In Brazil's box, Osley, Laird and Brian Brazil went up for the head ball against four Brazilian defenders and the goalkeeper. As the ball floated in the air, Brian Brazil got up higher in the air than anyone else. He made strong contact with the ball, hitting it downwards toward the ground. As the ball sailed down, it picked up speed and went past the extended arms of the Brazilian goalkeeper. England 1, Brazil 0. The English players celebrated this goal as a team. Brian Brazil ran towards his own sideline where Robbie Kiel and the rest of the team waited for him with open arms. Hugs and encouragement was all over the place as they celebrated Brazil's goal. England was doing it again. They were up by one going into the halftime against the best in the world.

Kiel, at halftime, "men, we started off slowly. But we picked up our play. I want everyone to listen to me with open ears. Whatever you have left in your gas tank, it's time to empty it out in the second half. The difference between winning and losing is one centimeter. Winners are those people who are willing to do what the others will not do. One centimeter to the left in your efforts, and you become a hero. One centimeter to the right in your efforts, and you become a ghost forever. For the next forty-five minutes, I want you to play the best football you ever played and become a legend. Because after those forty-five minutes, you can't ever replace this moment. Gentlemen, attention and execution make a perfect combination. Remember that, and enjoy the next forty-five minutes of your lives. You decide which one you want to become, a hero or a ghost."

The second half started off at a much faster pace than the first had. The Brazilians were ready to pull out all the stops to come back into the game. The Brazilian Samba Kings were peaking. They were getting the Brazilian crowd back into the game with heal passes, dribbling motions, easy flips of the ball, and the crowd loved it. In the fifty-third minute, the Brazilian striker received a perfect ball on the run without breaking his stride. He got to it and one touched a ball with his right foot towards the English goal. From where Robbie Kiel was standing, the ball was going in for sure. In the last second, the English captain dove back across his goal and made one of the greatest saves a goalkeeper could possibly make. People had seen Roark quick before, but no one had ever seen Roark react this quickly. The Brazilian striker thought it was in. So did 60,000 people. As soon as Roark made his amazing save, the Brazilian striker had an agonized look on his face.

Brazil's fast pace made the match become that much better. The game had all the makings of an instant classic. England was responding to the challenge. This was not the same team that had blown a lead four years ago and lost to Brazil. The Three Lions started playing tougher and stronger. They were playing mistake-free football. The crowd at Stadion Munchen loved the effort from the both sides. This was football at its best. In the seventieth minute, the game got a little testy. On a Brazilian corner kick, Roark had gone up for the ball and was undercut by the Brazilian forward. Roark went up and came back down on his back. The referee from Switzerland blew his whistle, awarding England with the foul. But Taggart, Osley, Landry and Brian Brazil wanted more than a yellow card. They wanted blood. The two teams began trading curse words and insults. Roark got up to let everyone know he was okay.

The next twenty minutes went even faster than the previous seventy for both teams. Brazil continued attacking with all of their available man power. Roark continued saving the raining shots by the Brazilian national team. These two teams were like two heavyweight boxers. Neither team willing to give an inch to the other. The Brazilian national team was throwing their best punches, and England was counter punching to the best of their ability. They, too, were attacking to put the game out of Brazil's reach. In the eighty-eighth minute, the Samba Kings attacked as an entire team against England. Brazil was outside of the English box and they took a shot. The ball went straight toward Roark. He did not try to catch this ball. The ball simply had too much power and velocity. Instead of catching the ball, Roark punched it over his own goal. The corner kick was awarded to Brazil. Brazil crowded the English box with ten men in the eighty-ninth minute.

> Roark was barking out orders; "Martin Taggart, get the front post! Landry, get the back post! Everyone else, grab yourself a Brazilian jersey."

Roark knew this was the most important moment of the semifinal game. The Brazilian mid-fielder crossed the ball into the English penalty area. The ball bounced once and then twice. It skidded amongst twenty men and found the Brazilian superstar's foot. He blasted a hard shot. Roark dove for it, but he could not get to it. The ball was going in. But Landry had not moved from his area during the corner kick at all. He saw Roark unable to stop the ball. Landry's reflexes took over. He dove after the ball as if he were the goalkeeper and made a diving catch. The referee immediately blew his whistle and pointed at the penalty area rewarding Brazil with a penalty kick. After awarding the kick, the referee turned to Landry and gave him his very well-deserved red card. No one, including Landry, argued with this call. For once, the referee had made the right call in the World Cup.

> As Landry walked off the field, Roark ran after him trying to console him; "John, you did the right thing. You gave us one more chance. That ball would have gone in if it wasn't for you. Don't worry about it, buddy. You did the right thing."

> Landry looked into Roark's concerned blue eyes and said, "remember what Kiel said, one centimeter either direction and you can be a ghost or a hero."

The Brazilian striker lined up to take the kick. He looked at Roark, and Roark looked back. The striker ran up to the ball and softly put the ball to the right side of the goal. Roark had studied this striker on videotape and knew which side he liked the most. Roark had picked his side and dove towards the direction he had already committed. With one sweeping motion, England was in the finals of the World Cup for the first time in forty years. Roark had done it again. He had made all the saves and all the plays necessary to win the World

Cup. At the final whistle of this game, the English players jumped in joy. They celebrated one of their biggest victories ever.

In the locker room, everyone was on cloud nine and then Kiel spoke, "it is a privilege and honor to be a part of this group, men. You have proven to me over and over again that there is no quit in this team. I am lucky to be part of a team like this. As I speak, I am getting goose bumps. I have three game balls to hand out."

Every one in the room was excited. Kiel got three balls from his equipment manager and called out the players' names.

Kiel, "the first one goes to Brian Brazil. Excellent goal."

Brazil hugged his coach; "thank you, sir." Everyone clapped and made cat-calls.

Kiel, "the second one goes to Josh Roark."

Josh walked up to his coach and he, too, gave him a hug; "thank you, Coach." Catcalls were raining on Roark.

Kiel, laughing as he spoke, "last, but definitely not least, who would have known how this game could have turned out if it wasn't for our back-up goalkeeper, John Landry? He did what he needed to do for us to win this match. I am proud of you, John. If it wasn't for you, Lord only knows what would have happened."

Landry also gave his coach a big hug; "thanks, Coach."

Kiel turned back to his troops and screamed as hard as he could, "one more win, and the Lions will roar again!!"

The English locker room exploded with chants of "one more game!" They had three days to get ready to play Germany in Berlin.

The day after England's victory over Brazil, the newspapers had many different headlines in England; one of the more clever ones read "Brazil beats Brazil." Others were good, but not as nearly as good, "Landry's hand saves England," "Roark is Charlton," "Kiel for Prime Minister."

Back in Germany, Kiel was still giving interviews about the Brazil game a day after the match had taken place.

William Thacker, "Sir Kiel, amazing performance. What were you thinking as The Brazilian superstar took that penalty kick?"

Kiel, "I was scared. He is an outstanding spot kicker. But we got lucky."

Mr. Thacker, "what do you think about John Landry's hand ball?"

Kiel, "it was the right thing to do. It gave us another chance to finish the game in regulation instead of going to overtime."

Mr. Thacker, "what can you say about Josh Roark?"

Kiel, "he is the heart and soul of this team. He has come up with so many big saves it is unbelievable."

Mr. Thacker, "what are your chances against Germany?"

Kiel, "Germany is strong everywhere. They have Ryan Grutch in defense and he is a beast back there. In the midfield they have David Rasmussen. He is like a bee, always producing. Up front they have Stefan Thonissen. You know he is the leading goal scorer of this World Cup, as of today. He is scary. We will give our best effort, but we are playing against the best football country in the world."

Mr. Thacker, "good luck, sir. Thank you very much for the interview."

CHAPTER 50

❀

† World War III

June 9, 2006 Germany. An hour before the World Cup final showdown between two of the most storied football countries of all time, it began to rain at Olympiastadion in Berlin. However, no amount of rain in the world could stop the 76,000 fans from attending the game. Many celebrities attended the much anticipated game, including actors, musicians, tennis stars, rugby stars and some former football legends from both countries. Beckenbauer and Charlton were at Olympiastadion in their private seats ready to show their support for their nation. Five minutes before the start of the match, Sir Robbie Kiel pulled his people together in the locker room. Every member of the English squad was together in a close circle waiting for Kiel to speak. He entered the circle wearing his favorite black suit with the Three Lions emblem on it.

> Sir Robbie Kiel addressed the team; "I am not going to lie to you, men. I am excited. I am nervous. I have puked three times in the past fifteen minutes, and I am shaking all over. I can't stop shaking. I wish I was out there with you guys, playing and contributing like I could have back in the day. But I can't. Time has played its dirty tricks on me. When I was a kid I never thought I would get old. I know some of you are thinking that I am not old. But in football years I am just an ancient memory. Now we have a chance to do something that has only been done once before us in England. It was forty years ago when the Three Lions truly roared. It was Charlton, Moore and Banks who brought the cup to England. Forty years

later we have Roark, Brazil and Harrison. Will you go down in the history of English football like your predecessors?"

Kiel stopped talking for a second and stared at his boys. He looked carefully at each one and then continued speaking.

Kiel, "I have never been this close with a team in my entire career. I look at us as a family, and I expect nothing but the best for and from this family. I want you to go out there in the next ninety minutes and play the best football that you ever played. I trust you, and I know you will do well. Needless to say, win or lose, I will always love each and every one of you as I love my own family. I love you guys, and you will always be champions in my book."

Kiel stopped speaking, and the team said a quick prayer together. They had on their red away jerseys, and they were ready to face the best team in the world.

The match at Olympiastadion started off at an amazing pace. Both teams were ready to take the lead early on. In the eleventh minute, the German libero, Ryan Grutch, started an attack from his defense by sending a long ball to his mid-fielder David Rasmussen. Rasmussen chested the ball in the air and brought it down. He looked up and saw the World Cups leading scorer, Stefan Thonissen, and sent him a perfect ball to the outside of the eighteen. Thonissen, upon receiving the ball, did not waste a second. He moved the ball to his right foot and took a shot. His line drive stayed low, and Roark made a diving attempt to stop it from going in. He had knocked the ball out in the last second. The German crowd was cheering for the host nation. Ten minutes later, Brian Brazil received a quick pass on the right side of the midfield from Roark. He looked up and recognized an opening in the midfield area and started dribbling the ball very quickly. The German mid-fielder, Rasmussen, challenged him, but Brazil went around him with ease. Brazil continued running with the ball as another German player challenged him, but Brazil made an amazing move and burned him, too. He was twenty-four yards out and gaining more speed as he ran. Another German challenged him but Brazil, in Maradonna-like fashion, went around this player with ease as well. Ryan Grutch was the last person to beat. As they started running shoulder to shoulder, Grutch threw an elbow at Brazil's stomach, but Brazil was too strong to be bumped off of the ball with a silly elbow. Brazil sped past Grutch, and, suddenly, he was one-on-one with the Bayern Munich's superstar goalkeeper. Brazil saw him coming out and blasted a shot that found the German net. Olympiastadion's English crowd exploded in cheers. England, like in many of their other World Cup games, started off by scoring quickly. England 1, Germany 0.

Brian Brazil scored his magical goal and ran as fast as he could with whatever energy he had left to the English fans. He put his index finger up to let them know this was his game. The English fans were going crazy. They had not seen a one man effort like this in years. The English fans started chanting the name of Brian Brazil for the next two minutes. Germany was one of the best teams in this World Cup, and they were not scared of one goal. Grutch, Rasmussen and Thonissen started playing stronger and more physically after the English goal. Thonissen and Rasmussen found each other every chance they had. In the thirty-eighth minute, Germany was awarded a corner kick. David Rasmussen would take the kick. Ryan Grutch had moved up forward to the England box for an opportunity to use his massive six feet four inch frame. Rasmussen took the kick, and Grutch went up for the ball. Taggart and Osley challenged Grutch's header. Grutch went up and made amazing contact with ball. The ball stayed low, and at the last possible second, Josh Roark made a diving catch. The German fans were disappointed, but they appreciated their libero's effort. The Germany versus England match went back and forth for the rest of the first half. The rain had picked up, and the players started sliding all over the field. The rain could not bring the high level of football down one bit. The crowd was in love with both team's extraordinary efforts. The first half came to an end with England leading Germany one to zero.

> At halftime, Josh Roark talked to everybody in the locker room, "come on guys, we have to answer the bell. They are coming from everywhere. We have to put a body on these ass holes. We have to start playing our brand of football. We can't let these pricks dictate what we want to do. We have to pick up our game. We have to pick up our intensity. They are playing at a high level. We have to turn our level up higher. We are going to win this game, and you have to pay attention to detail and execute properly to be the best in the world."

Everyone listened as the captain spoke to them. Sir Robbie Kiel, like everyone else, was listening to Roark speak and enjoying the moment. He knew years earlier when he had met this guy that he was different. He knew he had a winner.

> Roark continued his speech; "gentlemen, I want to remember the last forty-five minutes of my career as the best forty-five minutes of my life.

This is it for me. This is my last game playing football. I want you to know that I have never enjoyed playing football this much until I had the opportunity play with you amazing players. This team is amazing, and I hope we will play our best so some of us can go out as the World Cup champions."

Sir Robbie Kiel knew this news would come sometime after the World Cup. He loved Roark's logic. Sir Robbie Kiel knew these men would never let their modest captain go out as a loser. They would fight, claw, bite and do everything in their power to win one for the classiest person ever.

The second half started and the football level had risen to amazing heights from both sides. Germany attacked mercilessly; they needed a goal. In the forty-eighth minute, David Rasmussen took shot from the left side of the eighteen. The ball hit left his foot and headed towards the left side of the English goal. With one motion, Roark had made another diving save with ease. He got up quickly and found John Landry's replacement, Patrick Mason, on the left side. He threw the ball towards Mason, and the Three Lions countered rapidly. Mason found Wade in the midfield. Wade stopped, looked up and saw Laird right next to him. He gave Laird a short pass and Laird one touched the ball to an attacking Mason on the left side. Mason caught up with the ball and made a cross to the German penalty area. The German goalkeeper easily went up in the air and brought the ball down. He immediately sent a quick throw to Rasmussen, and Germany attacked again. In the seventy-fifth minute, Germany started coming from every corner of the field. Grutch received the ball in the center of the midfield and dribbled. Wade challenged him, and Grutch made a quick pass to Rasmussen. Rasmussen looked up and found another German defender making a run. As soon as the defender got to the ball, he had taken a shot. It was a rocket that sailed over the English goal. England did not play skittishly or carefully. They attacked. They were trying to finish the game on a high note.

The last ten minutes of this amazing World Cup Final went by quickly with both teams attacking as if the end of the world was near. Rasmussen continued shooting from every angle he had. In the eighty-seventh minute, Rasmussen took another hard shot. This time Roark dove for it and bobbled the ball for a second in front of him. Stefan Thonissen was in front of Roark and took a hard shot from ten yards away. The entire crowd stood still. The ball went higher and higher. Thonissen had missed a sure chance to tie the amazing match. All Thonissen should have done was place the ball in the corner of the British goal, instead he had used all his strength. The English fans and the Three Lions breathed in a collective sigh of relief. Germany knew this was their last chance to get back in the game.

In the ninetieth minute, the fourth referee from the sidelines raised a sign that said two more minutes of additional time. Germany tried to attack but England was there defending successfully each time. English fans at Olympiastadion were blowing their whistles in order for the game to finish. Finally, the head referee blew his whistle and pointed at the midfield area. The unforgettable match between Germany and England was over. Time had finally run out on the World Cup host. The Three Lions sideline cleared and everyone started running at one another in celebration. Roark hugged Taggart, Osley, Mason and Correal at the same time. Then, all of a sudden, Brazil, Laird, Harrisson and the rest of the England squad jumped on top of Roark. There was a big pile of English winners. Sir Robbie Kiel stood motionless at the sideline in disbelief while his assistant coaches congratulated him. The English crowd chanted until they lost their voices that evening. Sir Robbie Kiel cried as he watched his troops celebrate the victory of a lifetime. Josh Roark had received the Adidas Golden Ball for the most outstanding player in the World Cup. The Three Lions had done it. Forty years after Charlton in 1966, the Three Lions were finally able to roar again as the kings of the football world.

CHAPTER 51

❀

† Conclusion

Katie Roark knew this day would eventually come. She would face Josh, Robbie and her past. She would have to tell the truth to the only two men she had ever loved. She had waited twenty-six years to tell both of these men. She pondered for days after England had won the World Cup about the right time. What would she say to Josh? What would she say to Robbie? How would they take this extraordinary news? Would they be angry? Would they hate her? Would Josh hate Robbie? Would Josh think his mother was a whore? Would Robbie and Josh still be great friends? She worried about the answer to all of these questions. Then, one day at her house when Josh had come over with his wife, Lisa, and his little son, Bobby, she decided to tell her secret to both of these men at the same time.

Josh, "Mother, are you okay?"

Katie, "I am fine."

Josh, "are you sure?"

Katie, "yes my, little king."

Robbie, "Josh is right, honey; you don't look too well."

Katie, "I am fine. I want both of you to promise me something."

Robbie and Josh at the same time, "what is wrong?"

Katie, "no matter what I tell you now, promise me you will both forgive me for what I have done."

Robbie hugged his nervous wife; "no matter what it is, I will always love you, Katie."

Josh, "Mother, whatever it is, it won't change anything."

Katie, to both Robbie and Josh, "promise me!"

Robbie "I promise!"

Josh, "I promise, Mother."

Katie turned to Josh and said, "Robbie Kiel is your real father." Then she turned to her frozen husband as she held his cold hands and said, "Josh is your son."

978-0-595-82356-7
0-595-82356-4

Printed in the United States
43705LVS00007B/16-48

9 780595 823567